ANTIQUITY

THE COPERNICUS CHRONICLES

ANTIQUITY

Written and Created by: *Alfred Anthony*

Illustrations By: Husen A.A.

A DeVillacian Enterprises Production

TABLE OF CONTENTS

ANTIQUITY

REVELATIONS OF WAR

DENOUEMENT

<u>PREFATORY</u>

Who are you? Where does your allegiance lie? Your family? Your beliefs? Are they nestled deeply in your religion, or anchored in your political leanings? Or are you free-floating, with a disdainful neglect for both? For many, it's the home—or the land—they are defending, believing it to be something they can claim, rightfully and willfully. Yet for any of these, the question remains: How deeply do the bloodlines within you flow, giving you the confidence to stake your loyalty in something?

Or, to simplify: *Who are you?* - Have you always been yourself, or have you been molded and shaped by what the world has told you? For most, there is no choice. You are who you are, and perhaps, you've always been this way. To be clear: I am not speaking of destiny. No, this identity you clutch so tightly was constructed— built by the world around you, pieced together from the memories buried deep within your mind.

Ask yourself: Do you remember the beginning? Not just your beginning, but the beginning of all that surrounds you. Search deeply—look carefully. You may encounter it in a dream or stumble upon it in the haze of a distant memory. Regardless, it's there—I swear it. Open the door to your full mind, for only there will you find the answers you seek. Not just your beginning, but the beginning of life itself. The moment when humanity took its first step. And when you reach that place, you will finally understand why you've fought so hard to truly *be* you.

War is a patient spectator, waiting on the fringes. It stands ready to pounce the moment you start asking yourself: *Is this my home? My land? My planet?* That's when war begins to stir within you, seizing the opportunity to surface. Suddenly, fighting for who you are—and for what you believe to be true—becomes your reason for existing. Those who yield to this call often rise as leaders. They search, preach, and prey upon others with similar beliefs, drawing strength from familiarity and resonance. Leaders possess the unique power to awaken the need for war within their followers, amplifying that inner struggle for preservation.

But what if there is no *right* or *wrong*? What if there are only beliefs—the things that resonate within each of us, whether born, bred, or taught? Beliefs are what compel us to take a stand at some point. From the soul comes purpose, for the soul defines you. It absorbs infinitely and arrives as a clean slate. It is vast, like the universe—boundless, yet minuscule. It holds beliefs yet begins without them. You are better off not resisting it but welcoming it. Listen to the soul's questions, even though it offers few answers. It is your *Antiquity*— the beginning and end of you. It holds the truths you would be willing to die for.

Many people believe in a pivotal moment—a single point in time worth staking everything on. But hear me: Life is not built on one moment. It is built on every moment, none more significant than the others. Moments are the building blocks of life, each one essential for the next step. We cannot move forward without looking back, and we cannot look back unless we've already moved forward. So, take a look around you. Some of the moments you seek have already passed, quietly propelling you forward, though they may not have revealed their importance just yet. Other moments are more obvious—sometimes appearing to be the inception of something new, when in truth, they are merely a chapter in a much older story.

Everything that has happened serves as a reference, lesson or a warning, teaching us how to avoid the traps of history. Yet history, over time, becomes lost in translation. It decays slowly as it is passed from one generation to the next, until one day, it is regarded only as a distant story, a legend, or a myth.

I am here to speak of history. To truly understand where we stand now, we must journey back and examine why our motherland fell—yet again. My hope is that this time, we can achieve greater success than in our past attempts. Why did beliefs and knowledge, once unified, diverge? How did these practices—synonymous across generations—break from the continuity of inherited traditions, only to splinter along the way? It may seem naïve to think this way, but I stand firm in my belief: understanding this rupture could save our species.

In what follows, significant names and places will surface, though they can no longer be confirmed, or proven memory is our only anchor. Much of it has already begun to decay, lost in the long passage through generations. Yet I implore you, reader, to accept them as truth. Like Earth's Apostles— whether from the first wave or the second (or for those of biblical persuasion, the second and third)—names and identities are often immortalized to mark their stories and secure their impact. Consider also the Guardians of Mars, the Hexcorebots, and our earliest builders of historical regions. Think of Jacob and his father, Peter, and their legacy. And do not forget the new worlds: Fortuna, along with its neighboring planet, Bacchus.

Legend and hearsay demand careful handling, especially now that both Goliath and David have presumably been destroyed, and the precise coordinates of the universe have slipped into myth, fading from humanity's grasp. Some whispered that before the High Fortunates were executed, they engraved these coordinates somewhere within the Expedites' convoy. But most dismiss this as mere legend—just as they do the idea that any true High Fortunates might still exist among us on this caravan. Yet I tell you, reader, the story that follows is as close to the truth as we can hope to get.

Though this tale is as ancient as time itself, it must be told again. This epoch, though just a fragment of the universe, holds immense significance. History is always unfolding, and if we close our eyes, it will repeat itself. Whether we view it through the lens of the past or under new light, the truth will remain unchanged. **Iasol 1:1**

"THE AGE OF ALLIANCES"

IN THE BEGINNING

In what was believed to be near the second or third decade of Earth's calendar—around the year 2000 AD, as recorded by the old Julian calendar—an asteroid was observed hurtling toward Earth. This was just a few short years before the much-prophesied alignment of the stars on December 21, 2012, AD, marking the so-called ascension of Earth. The asteroid entered the solar system, passing beyond Neptune and Pluto, lingering quietly in the outer reaches. At first, its arrival caused little concern; its initial trajectory was alarming, but once it stabilized and ceased to approach Earth, it garnered only mild scientific interest.

Still, there was something peculiar about this celestial body. It wasn't like other meteorites that had previously burned through Earth's atmosphere or drifted through space unnoticed. Unfortunately, much of what happened in those early days was lost during the Day of Decimation, when countless records were destroyed. What we know now is based on stories handed down through generations.

There were no official ledgers, only whispers, and fragments of accounts scattered across time. The asteroid's appearance was noted in a few obscure scientific journals and even less significant literary works—documents most people overlooked. However, the Scrolls of Jacob, a narrative compiled after Earth's rebirth, seems to confirm that the asteroid's arrival was real, even if few recognized its significance at the time.

Governments concealed much about the asteroid from the public. Its sheer size and strange characteristics raised concerns among officials, but they assured citizens that there was no immediate threat. Authorities insisted they would only release information once they better understood the object's nature, hoping to avoid panic. In truth, nothing like this had ever been documented in human history—at least, not in any surviving records. Still, officials clung to the belief that this encounter was nothing more than a rare cosmic occurrence, one that could be explained by the vast, unpredictable nature of the universe.

Unfortunately, they were wrong. Catastrophically wrong.

I must pause here to reiterate the scarcity of reliable records from that time. Documentation was deliberately limited by those in power to manage public perception, and what little remained was destroyed in the chaos of later events. As a result, much of what follows is pieced together from conflicting accounts. The use of multiple calendars only complicates the matter, making it difficult to establish exact dates. But the Scrolls of Jacob offer the clearest, most reliable glimpse into these events. For this reason, I am inclined to believe they contain the closest version of the truth.

As the asteroid continued to hover in the solar system, we now call Copernicus, a handful of advanced observers began to realize it was not just a lifeless rock but a highly sophisticated vessel. Its exterior, coated in rock-like formations and shimmering minerals, had been deceptive. Beneath that facade lay advanced technology. It remained stationary for a time, seemingly content to drift in place. What was it waiting for? And more importantly, what had it accomplished during its silent watch over the Copernican solar system? But without consistent information being supplied along with other newsworthy distractions, Panspermia began to fade from the eyes and minds of the public. Just as so many other moments throughout history have done in the past. Until one day Panspermia had awoken again, and this time could not be ignored as it made its way toward planet Earth.

It soon became evident that the asteroid was not a natural formation but an alien craft, a massive carrier transporting life forms from another world. The icy crust and crystalline surface that had initially disguised it were revealed to be exposed machinery, mechanisms unlike anything Earth had ever seen. The craft was vast—over 13 miles long, 2 miles wide, and towering the equivalent of a ten-story building. A protrusion jutted from its underside, distinct from the rest of the craft's rocky exterior, hinting at a complex structure beneath. The ship's surface shimmered under the sunlight, reflecting like a crystal, though this was merely an illusion—its true form was a fusion of machinery and biology, a living environment capable of traversing the stars.

It wasn't just a vessel. It was a transport for a mysterious species, known in Earth's mythology as the Fortunates. The ship's design was so advanced that it blurred the line between mineral and mechanism, living organism and machine. Though some theorized that part of the exterior might have crystallized naturally, the shimmering surface only masked the ship's true nature. Eventually, Earth's inhabitants learned the name of this extraordinary vessel: Panspermia.

That name —Panspermia— would come to define a significant era in human history. It was more than a ship or transport by any stretch of the imagination. It was a mass of land, traveling through space at incomprehensible speeds until it arrived at its destination.

Its arrival, so to speak, marked what became known as the Year of Unsettling for the people of Earth. There was no longer any way to keep it hidden. Despite leadership's best efforts to calm nerves and dispel rumors, Earth's inhabitants filled the unknown with a litany of beliefs, customs, and speculations. Religious theories regarding the end of days gave way to chaos in some places—crime spiked, and controlled mayhem simmered on the surface.

This unprecedented visitation from an otherworldly entity shattered millennia of human understanding about the space beyond their planet. All eyes were now fixed on the vessel idling between Mars and Earth. Suddenly, humanity realized it was not alone. While the notion of life beyond Earth may have always been a distant thought, Panspermia confirmed it— with an exclamation mark.

The question weighing on every mind was now an unavoidable one: What comes next?

Panspermia

Panspermia first settled outside of Mars, or at least that's where it was officially recorded as being discovered and acknowledged by Earth's populace. However, its initial sighting occurred long before this event.

The entity streaked through space, initially mistaken for a comet or meteor by scientists who lacked any other explanation for this massive land formation infiltrating our solar system. As it entered, it decelerated and settled in the far reaches of the outer planets. It was then that they realized it was something far more extraordinary.

The way light reflected off its surface revealed what first appeared to be water fragments or ice pieces to be, in fact, metal and glass—a revelation that defied their current understanding. Scientists theorized that organisms had attached themselves to the rock as it journeyed through the galaxy, though none knew for how long or how far it had traveled. This concept, too, was beyond their comprehension. The entity appeared to be alive, thriving on the exterior of what was once thought to be a simple celestial body.

Most of Earth's population was kept in the dark about its initial penetration into the solar system. Years after its first entry, when it began a second movement at an unprecedented speed with uncanny smoothness, scientists were once again baffled. It clearly wasn't a comet or any celestial object they were familiar with. Over the years, theories emerged, with some individuals showing more interest and concern than others. Despite this, most investigative studies had been suppressed. However, when it finally settled just outside Mars' orbit, there was no way to keep its existence from the public or ignore its complexity and the profound implications it held for Earth's inhabitants.

The mass extended approximately thirteen miles in length and over two miles in width. What was once considered to be organisms or life-like entities on its exterior was now confirmed to be intricate structures of glass and metal protruding from within—a tantalizing glimpse of what lay beneath the terraformed surface. As it remained dormant outside Mars for just over a month, it became evident that an extraterrestrial visitor had arrived.

Earth's populace reacted with a spectrum of emotions, ranging from reverence to apocalyptic fear. Some became worshippers, while others believed the end of the world was imminent. Regardless of individual reactions, one thing was certain: this mysterious visitor occupied the thoughts of every person on Earth.

That name —*Panspermia*— would come to define a significant era in human history. It was more than a ship or transport by any stretch of the imagination. It was a mass of land, traveling through space at incomprehensible speeds until it arrived at its destination.

Its *arrival*, so to speak, marked what became known as the Year of *Unsettling* for the people of Earth. There was no longer any way to keep it hidden. Despite leadership's best efforts to calm nerves and dispel rumors, Earth's inhabitants filled the unknown with a litany of beliefs, customs, and speculations. Religious theories regarding the end of days gave way to chaos in some places—crime spiked, and controlled mayhem simmered on the surface.

This unprecedented visitation from an otherworldly entity shattered millennia of human understanding about the space beyond their planet. All eyes were now fixed on the vessel idling between Mars and Earth. Suddenly, humanity realized it was not alone. While the notion of life beyond Earth may have always been a distant thought, *Panspermia* confirmed it—with an exclamation mark.

The question weighing on every mind was now an unavoidable one: What comes next?

THE SUMMONING

That question was soon answered by the visitors. Within the *Scrolls of Jacob*, an initial meeting of six heads of nations and the leadership of Panspermia commenced and concluded. However, the inception and cessation of this meeting were far more complex than anyone could have imagined. Everything that transpired from the moment of contact to its conclusion had such a profound impact on the people of Earth—some would even say it was traumatizing—that it was documented and repeated countless times, eventually being regarded as the beginning of the end.

Yet, this significance was not realized at the time. Historical events are rarely understood as pivotal in the moment they unfold; their true importance is revealed only in the aftershocks. Even the initial contact was etched in the minds of those who witnessed it, leading them to question whether what they had seen had truly happened. Panspermia sought a rather alarming form of communication with Earth.

In less than ten minutes local time, a beam of light stretched from Panspermia to Earth, engulfing the planet in a hazy sheet of light and power. Then, an image emerged—one that felt less like a vision and more like synchronized thought. At the sight of it, Earth's inhabitants erupted into hysteria. The light radiated power, casting the image across the sky for all to witness, but it was within their minds that the image truly manifested. And then, he appeared.

Adom's presence spread across the sky, visible to all of humankind. According to the scriptures, the sheer magnitude of the image and the clarity of the sound that accompanied it created an otherworldly experience, reminiscent of divine encounters described in religious lore. The message Adom delivered through this vision was perfectly synchronized with his voice, as though the two were inseparable. His voice resonated clearly in every mind, as if their thoughts had been overtaken by his presence, revealing Adom's face deep within their consciousness as he spoke.

Adom's tone was warm and welcoming as he addressed the people of Earth. He was mindful of the intimidating figure he presented and the impact of his sudden, overwhelming arrival. The image hovering in the sky may have seemed shocking—if not outright terrifying—but that was not how he wanted this moment to be perceived. He needed the people to hear him, truly hear him. In his request for an assembly with world leaders, Adom imposed no deadlines or ultimatums. Instead, he offered an extension of respect and an invitation.

In the faded, fragmented translation of *Jacob's Scrolls*, the following excerpt is the closest record of Adom's words. Although the original message was said to last nearly ten minutes, much of it has been lost to time and the destruction of records. What remains is the recollection of those who either summarized it with careful intent or simply remembered the words that resonated most deeply:

'Do not fear me, inhabitants of Earth. I am Adom, and we are not here to be part of your demise, but rather to help. You are ascending from the darkest day of the iron age, and we are here to guide you. Earth is about to witness a permitted and accelerated passage to enlightenment—the beginning of a soul rising to become one with the universe. We seek for you to achieve heights never before seen on this planet. It is peace, it is knowledge, it is immortality. Please now have me meet with the leaders of the following lands...' —*Jacob's Scrolls*

Adom

His name was Adom, and he hailed from Fortuna. Although he was merely the messenger and voice of the Fortunates, no one was more significant to this pivotal moment on Earth. His selection was deliberate, not accidental. Several factors contributed to this appointment, including his charm and mannerisms. He had a unique ability to make everyone not only understand but, in his cunning way, believe everything he said. His words were always accompanied by logic and a smile. While the logic he articulated was sound, there was often an ulterior motive behind his actions and words. The Fortunates needed to ensure that their intentions remained undiscovered and, more importantly, unopposed.

When Adom appeared, his features and stature resembled those of the humans populating Earth at the time, making his figure familiar to them—except for his complexion. His head had a metallic appearance with a chrome finish, but he was not a robot. A more fitting description, or at least how the Earthlings would likely have categorized him, was as a cyborg. However, his nature was far more complex and unfamiliar to them than that. His cranium generated what the Fortunates referred to as micro-biotic cells. These cells resulted from advanced micro-engineering, reproducing within the cranium and extending down through the spine, which lay beneath the skin just as it does in all humans. However, the micro-biotic cells could be dispensed throughout if needed. His skin, somewhat transparent, allowed glimpses of the coursing blood beneath, creating an aberration of sorts. It actually glowed with a crimson hue. The micro-biotics would regenerate any damaged cells they encountered, attaching themselves and restoring them to wholeness. This same engineering was consistent among all the Fortunates; the only difference lay in the glow of their exterior. While Adom exhibited a crimson glow, another, such as Echo, would display a bluish tint. It was later theorized that the intensity of the glow correlated with the amount and usage of the micro-biotic cells for repairs, contributing to the Fortunates' near immortality—well, almost.

Another reason Adom was chosen was his mastery of Baccha, an obscure science learned by some back on Fortuna, but none had achieved the depth and magnitude that Adom had attained. He possessed the remarkable gift of communicating with his mind to others, producing electric waves that stimulated the recipients' minds, allowing them to hear him speak within their consciousness. Furthermore, he could project images, which were essential for conveying messages that all Earthlings needed to receive. While others in the high court were capable of this, none could match Adom's magnitude; he could perform this feat not just for one or a few, but for billions at once.

While his speech during The Summoning and his calming presence during the Seven Days of Destruction through Baccha will always be remembered, they pale in comparison to the recorded words he spoke aloud on the Tune to Ajax and an unknown individual who would later be revealed as one of Earth's own:

"Purification of all is what we need to do, and if that means genocide, then so be it. It will ensure the balance of the universe so that we never fall victim to plummeting into the dark again."

How he rose to such prominence in the high courts of Tropacion alongside Icon remains uncertain, but it is assumed that Icon recognized his talents and was eager to utilize them. A war was raging back on Fortuna, and it was a war that was being lost; they needed a plan, and Adom would become a significant part of that strategy. Hearing him speak was both harmonious and hypnotic. While Baccha allowed for communication and the creation of mental images, it did not mean one could manipulate another's mind. That required charm.

Following this explanation, the names of the six nations were announced, along with instructions on where the leaders should assemble for their eventual journey to the vessel still stationed near Mars—what was known as Panspermia. First, however, they were to board a transport that the visitors would send to the surface of Earth, eventually known as the Tune.

The Tune

A marvel all unto its own was *The Tune*. From the moment it ascended from Panspermia to its arrival at 0:0, the people of Earth gazed upon it with awe. After Adom announced the leaders' summoning, a less intimidating conveyance was sent to Earth to transport the officials back to Panspermia. It moved with the speed and agility reminiscent of its origin, but it was a domed city that glistened brightly as it streaked towards its rendezvous point.

Adom had explained that it would settle at 0:0—the coordinates of Earth's zero latitudes and zero longitudes, where the Equator crossed the Prime Meridian. The point was chosen, he elaborated, to symbolize the equality of all lands in the eyes of his people; this was the center of their world. It was also situated in the middle of the Atlantic Ocean, but that was no issue for this marvel. The sophisticated machinery that would settle below the ocean was an irrigation system designed to draw water from the sea, a feat of engineering that would later serve the region then known as Cameroon, destined to be called Alliance Pointe in Labryanthia.

Inside, the marvel known as The Tune—also named after one of the first Viking ships of Old Earth—was even more magnificent than it appeared from a distance. Structures of soft steel, gold-plated buildings, and astounding plant life welcomed the guests. If they only knew that this was just the beginning of their amazement. Upon entering its host ship, Panspermia, the dome would seamlessly integrate into Panspermia interior, equal in beauty to The Tune but vastly different from its exterior of rock and dirt.

This location would be identified as 0:0. History tells us that it was, indeed, a latitude and longitude position on the surface of Earth. Yet it lay in the vast blue seas of the planet, where leaders were to gather in a land then known as Cameroon. It would later become the legendary home of Apostles I, referred to as the Apostles Hall—all in due time. Still, so much more needed to be told before that occurred, and to disclose it ahead of time would not aid the history that must be remembered.

The lands known at the time as the United States, China, Russia, United Kingdom, Brazil, and Egypt were requested to send representatives to meet with Adom. Although the names of those leaders may be recorded somewhere, it was the specifics of the lands that would ultimately have a significant impact during the days known as *The Seven Days of Destruction* and later during the restructuring of what were the seven continents into the U.L.E. (United Lands of Earth).

His euphonious yet assertive voice echoed throughout the planet, captivating attention and cementing a sense of dominance. This announcement would soon be referred to as *the Summoning*. A perfect portrait against the faded and indistinguishable background, the chrome head and metallic yet almost transparent extremities of Adom were both alarming and beautiful. While the reasons behind this specific assembly of regions and lands remained unclear to Earth, Adom had painstakingly chosen each location for precise reasons.

More details surround the event and the subsequent rallying of these nations' leaders, but no accounts of combat or attack from either side exist. Given the circumstances, a normal military movement and precautionary response were anticipated. However, the inhabitants of Earth quickly realized that an attempt to resist or retaliate against their advanced visitors would most likely be futile.

An apportioned piece of Panspermia disconnected from the vessel and moved swiftly toward the chosen rendezvous location. The once-thought crystallization protruding from the center was merely the bottom of the transport. The dome above was a vision to behold, unlike any craft the dwellers of Earth had ever witnessed.

Though the smaller piece moved quickly, given the distance, it arrived at the location nearly three Earth weeks later, settling comfortably on Earth's surface. The smaller extract from Panspermia appeared to be a simple dome, serving as an eco-vessel. It was far less intimidating than its originator, conveying a sense of non-threatening presence, much like the arrival of the Fortunates a month earlier. Once it fully arrived, it hovered, awaiting the fulfillment of Adom's request.

Nearby, a small city located in what was then known as the continent of Africa, but most recognize it as its more recently named land that would come to be known as Labryanthia filled with hundreds of officials from the six nations accompanying the leaders summoned to meet with Adom. This location would eventually be called "Alliance" and later become a settlement for the people of Earth. From one of the protrusions of the floating city, a piece detached itself from The Eco Dome and jettisoned across the ocean without ever touching the water. This craft, later referred to as The Barge, was preparing for contact with its expected passengers. Unaware of the craft's true nature, panic ensued among the people standing before it, but their fears subsided when a calming voice entered their minds—a voice of explanation. For 0:0 rested within the great South Atlantic Ocean, and this was merely a means of travel to the settled dome. While a hint of nervousness lingered until the Barge's arrival, most trusted the soothing words, and all they could do was wait.

For the first time since the arrival of Panspermia, the people of Earth witnessed their visitors in full form. Although a marvel to behold, the beings' size was not far from that of humans. Figures presumed to be soldiers of the escort adorned in armor showcased heads made of metal. At first glance, they resembled helmets, but it became apparent that what rested on their shoulders was a living organ, complete with facial features and expression. This group remained mostly stoic, absent of overt expression, yet they were integral parts of their visitors' bodies.

Unbeknownst to Earth at the time, the design of their skulls held significance—serving as anchors for a cell-generating machine. Despite their mechanical appearance, they were fully living and breathing beings, giving no impression of artificiality. Each soldier's skull was a different shade of gold, red, and silver, signifying rank. The Endicots, as they were called, were imposing figures, vastly different from anything Earth and its residents had encountered. Most quoted leaders and the forces accompanying them described feeling a tinge of apprehension and intimidation at the sight of their otherworldly visitors.

To ease their concerns, the leaders were permitted to bring their full details of protection and guardsmen aboard the Eco Pod as they were transported back to The Tune and eventually to Panspermia. As the Earthlings made their way toward the transport, the Endicots spoke no words, respectfully parting to create a path. A harmonious figure awaited them as they entered. This time, it was not Adom but another important Fortunate who introduced himself as Echo. His features closely resembled Adom's, but a faint blue tint graced his outer layer, and he wore a robe reminiscent of a religious figure. We would later learn the ways of the Fortunates and their beliefs, affirming their almost prophetic status.

Echo was known as a Historian in rank, where history served as their religion. Although he was not heavily guarded aside from the rows of Endicots lining the way toward him, one notable figure stood beside him—Ajax, a most famous Endicot. As Echo welcomed each leader in their native tongues, it became evident to the Earthlings that this was the calming voice they had heard earlier. This recognition made it much easier for them to proceed onward.

Upon entering the urban domed city, the leaders scanned their surroundings for any signs of threat or intimidation. Yet, even inside, the transport vehicle felt less frightening and more welcoming than expected. Greenery flourished, and park-like pathways invited them in. There were even rumors of bird-like inhabitants, though this was never confirmed, as tales passed down from generation to generation embellished the experience. However, one thing remained certain: the interior was not an imposing place, nor did it aim to intimidate its guests. It was a comforting habitat.

The length of the pod measured approximately 900 meters in circumference. As mentioned earlier, plant life created a breathable atmosphere, not merely generated by mechanical means; it was genuine. As the pod glided through the skies, an internal light illuminated the dome, independent of sunlight and seemingly without end.

Inside, small buildings rested low to the ground, crafted from a soft, metallic stone. The most prominent structure —a golden edifice— stood at around nine stories, occupying the center of the pod. Most assumed it served as a place of worship, though this was only confirmed years later when it became a venue for important meetings and homage to their home world, albeit on a smaller scale. The entire ambiance of the transport emanated a sense of holiness or sacredness, a welcome assurance for those venturing into the unknown.

AJAX

A formidable and intimidating presence was the Endicot known as Ajax. The Endicots, loyal soldiers of the Fortunate order, were engineered for protection and enforcement, and Ajax stood as their unyielding commander. If ranks were to be spoken of, he was an admiral—not merely a guardian, but a strategist intricately woven into every significant decision, including key tactical maneuvers and governance. Thus, earning him the right to occupy one of the six thrones within the walls of the Golden Tower.

Ajax was more imposing than the other Endicots, embodying the essence of their warrior lineage. Unlike the mirrored chrome of the Fortunates, his cranium bore a unique texture, a testament to the rigorous battles he had endured. His skin glimmered with a blackened and deep gray hue, a reflection of his past injuries, indicative of a life steeped in conflict. Each Endicot's head showcased a metallic sheen, but Ajax's distinguished platinum dome marked him as unparalleled—there was only one Ajax.

The *Vitality Sword* he wielded was no ordinary weapon. When energized, it allowed him to harness the very essence of vitality surrounding it. Each *Endicot* possessed a similar blade, but *Ajax's* was legendary. It could strike with diverse effects—from stunning and paralyzing foes to slicing through adversaries with lethal precision, and even projecting a scorching energy that could incinerate its target. Though all other *Endicot's Vitality Swords* possessed the same technological gifts, the might and strength of *Ajax's* were legendary. Whispers echoed through the ranks about the special nature of *Ajax's* sword, which he affectionately named *Jupiter*. It was said to rival the fabled *Excalibur* in renown across the lands.

Ajax played a pivotal role in numerous military campaigns and strategic operations, becoming a name known to many, even without the charismatic speeches of *Adom*. His presence alone commanded respect, and while he never addressed the crowds, his character spoke volumes. Unlike *Adom*, *Ajax's* silence held a weight that would resonate in the annals of history, forever linking his name to the infamous *Day of Decimation*.

As the domed vessel made its journey back to Panspermia, those aboard reported an extraordinary experience. Despite the rapid acceleration that might have appeared jarring from the outside, the passengers felt none of it. Inside, they moved freely and comfortably, unrestrained by the ship's speed. The thoughtfulness and care put into this visitation were evident, with officials and their security granted the utmost respect and comfort, alleviating the shock of their circumstances.

However, the same could not be said for those remaining on Earth.

THE SEVEN DAYS OF DESTRUCTION

Throughout the nearly three weeks of transport by the Tune back to its point of origin, speculation surged in key areas, igniting both protests and impassioned preachings that kept the Earthlings on high alert. At the time of Arrival, Old Earth was a patchwork of significant borders—heavily defended, clearly defined, and resulting in rampant divisions across its surface. While some borders were drawn for political reasons, many were a product of deep-rooted religious beliefs, shaping notions of morality and divinity that created stark separations: Earthling from Earthling, tribe from tribe.

Religion has a peculiar way of isolating its adherents; at times, it even provokes heated arguments among strangers. As the three weeks of transport progressed, Earthlings reached heightened levels of speculation and tension. Protests erupted, and self-proclaimed "truth-tellers" espousing "hidden truths" and "confirmed conspiracies" rang loudly through the streets. Across the Lands, factions fueled fears with their interpretations of the uncertain future, especially concerning those lands that had been represented and those left behind. The officials remaining with the represented Earthlings managed to regain control of most uprisings with relative ease. Threats of terrorism and waves of panic faded into a low, dull noise as the majority attempted to return to their normal routines.

Yet, the echo of unrest was louder in countries without representation. The absence of a seat at the table bred skepticism, causing the public and governments to question everything. Fear of exclusion, jealousy of their neighbors' advantages, and the rekindling of age-old resentments led villages and countrymen to turn against one another, demanding political action or social revolution. The 24-hour news cycle highlighted the worst of humanity, stoking fear and anxiety as rebel groups targeted their capitals and leadership. Military forces were mobilized, either to protect or, in many cases, to act against their own people. Thus, chaos began to unfold, as I have learned through stories passed down through generations.

Little documentation remains from this turbulent time; almost all texts were deemed unworthy of preservation. The true scale of destruction was unknown, and even the ancient Scrolls failed to record events from years before the rebellious activities commenced. Specifics varied widely from region to region, making accurate accounts nearly impossible. Religious wars over land rights and territory flared anew. Zealots from one faction infiltrated their enemies, detonating bombs or committing atrocities in the name of intolerance. Weaker cultures became targets of scorn for those who outnumbered them, as genocide and guerrilla warfare engulfed the jungles and shorelines of old religious territories. Ancient texts revealed that such wars had raged for centuries, if not millennia. In the absence of oversight, many took advantage of the chaos, reigniting the flames of controversy.

The greatest of these struggles unfolded in what was once known as the Middle East, now a small part of Paramatastan. The initial seven days of conflict, later termed "The Seven Days of Destruction," echoed a narrative from the Earthlings' holy text—the Bible—called the "Seven Days of Creation."

The earliest accounts passed down suggest that the first day brought a darkness that swallowed the skies. Several bombs rained down on major cities, filling the air with choking smoke that obscured the light of day. By the second day, the clouds had spread across the globe, suffocating lands far and near. On the third day, contamination poisoned both seas and land. The fourth day saw the Sun's rays entirely blotted out, eclipsed by the fallout, rendering even the moon and brightest stars invisible. Due to the environmental devastation, it was said that birds fell lifeless from the sky, and fish washed ashore in ghastly numbers. Wildlife perished in staggering quantities, and, tragically, countless lives were lost. By the seventh day, the landscape appeared deceptively calm, but this was merely a façade; fear and exhaustion gripped all who remained. These tales, recounted by elders claiming to have witnessed the destruction, raise questions about their accuracy and whether they held symbolic meaning. What is irrefutable, however, is the chaos that swept across the globe, leaving a desperate need for intervention. While exact death tolls remain elusive, estimates suggest hundreds of thousands perished during this catastrophic period.

As the visitors aboard the Tune began to receive clearer accounts of the turmoil back on Earth, panic swept through the leaders of the so-called "free world." Concern for the safety of their families, friends, and citizens ignited an urgent plea for their hosts to turn back. While the extraterrestrial visitors did not relent, Adom sought to quell the rising fear and chaos. Once again, he reached out to the people of Earth, a moment reminiscent of his arrival but lacking the visual spectacle of beams or images projected in the sky. Instead, a gateway opened in the minds of the Earthlings, revealing Adom's visage on a more subconscious level, leaving them to wonder if it had truly happened or if it was merely a figment of their imagination.

His message was clear and resonant:
"Please, good people of Earth. We did not come to create division and fear among you. I apologize for the turmoil and anguish caused, but you will soon see the truth. For all of this is not only for this moment but for purposes both now and in times to come. All will be explained."

With these words, a newfound sense of unfettered communication blossomed between the leaders aboard the Tune and their constituents back home. The chaos that had once plagued Old Earth began to wane, yielding to a collective sense of patience. Adom's ability to speak powerfully and compellingly had once again tamed the wild nature of the Earthlings. Regular updates depicted the care taken by their extraterrestrial visitors, gradually reshaping their image from formidable beings to affable and welcoming hosts.

However, lingering questions remained about the damage already inflicted. The days ahead would require urgent efforts to address the devastation wrought during the Seven Days of Destruction. It was evident that the Earthlings stood on the brink of war, their readiness palpable amidst the remnants of the Iron Age.

As the 24-hour news cycle continued, local media, scientists, and historians of Old Earth meticulously dissected Adom's speeches. Over time, even the staunchest naysayers found less evidence of alarm or imminent threat. The realization dawned that whatever was destined to occur would happen regardless of chaotic behavior. Gradually, thoughts of peace, unity, and prosperity replaced the warnings of sinister intentions. Even now, long after the events on Earth have concluded, the desire for peace and prosperity remains, echoing across the cosmos. Our people, too, search for this elusive tranquility, born from the ashes of a past marred by conflict and chaos.

AND THEN ADOM APPEARED

When the final day arrived and the Tune officially began its ascent into Panspermia, nearly all activity on Earth halted in anticipation. The leaders aboard disembarked and commenced an official meeting with Adom and the leaders of what would soon become a new and impressive world that Adom envisioned for them. Meanwhile, the

people on Earth watched in awe as the dome retracted, and the small city became part of the terraforming inside the vessel. The interior was nothing like its harsh rock-like exterior; it was highly advanced and pristine. Each nation had varied documented accounts of its encounter, with slight variations in details and key moments. Although cameras transmitted views back to Earth, all who were present would later claim that the magnetism and beauty of what they witnessed in person were beyond comprehension. They shared a common sense of a welcoming experience at the hands of this new community of beings. Some of the most detailed accounts were recorded in the "Scrolls," with the United Kingdom of Old Earth providing the most extensive narratives.

Then Adom appeared in the flesh, so to speak. He looked just as he had on his summoning day, more robotic in appearance due to science that Earthlings did not comprehend, yet undeniably a man. His blood coursed almost visibly through his skin, a series of micro-biotics attaching themselves to every cell. These micro-biotics assisted in the constant reconstruction of any damaged cells or diseases, making the body nearly immortal. As mentioned earlier, these micro-biotics stemmed from the metallic cranium that formed their skull. Without this astounding science, Adom and all other Fortunates would appear merely human in movement, expression, and speech. For the most part, Adom communicated with them telepathically, refraining from verbal speech—likely to avoid any language barrier constraints. When he did speak aloud, his dialect resembled Old English, infused with hints of an unfamiliar tongue.

The account of this encounter shared history with the Earthlings unlike anything ever told. While the masses could witness the meeting through Adom's Bacchian gift of the mind, the translation of his words was somewhat incomplete for those back on Earth—similar to someone switching in and out of their native language when speaking to multilingual groups. However, all government officials confirmed the content of his speech. It recounted the past and the scale of time that revealed the truth behind theories, beliefs, and mysteries that humanity had held for millennia. Clarity about their world emerged, along with a timeline of events. It was an astonishing conversation shared by Adom with the leaders of Earth, filling every gap of knowledge that had plagued humanity since its dawn—accurate accounts of beginnings, endings, and everything in between.

One notable revelation involved the Mayan calendar, an ancient mystery that had troubled Earthlings for centuries. Up to that point, inhabitants of Earth believed the calendar depicted a clear beginning and end. However, as Adom pointed out with pristine clarity, it was designed to portray the ebb and flow of the stars and the universe itself. He explained that the calendar experienced a peak followed by a valley every 13,000 years, illuminating Earth's "ages" of knowledge and darkness. When the calendar was created, earlier people recorded it, but it was lost through the ages—likely due to the alignment moving further from the Golden Age and the natural fading of history as stories became less accurately passed down through generations. Though people of Earth throughout the lands had fragments of their history, in truth the great puzzle was incomplete or misinterpreted as it passed through generations and voyaged around the globe. It was scattered and lost upon the people as the universe took its ever-evolving turns through the Ages. Along with the universe falling in and out of alignment the challenge became that much more causing the inhabitants to constantly begin anew. Thus, beliefs and information became dependent upon the storyteller or recipient that turned messenger only to contribute to its inconsistencies and cavernous gaps. It was presumed that Adom had put an end to all of that and was here to retell and enlighten the people about days past. During the Golden Age, people perceived the universe with greater clarity, becoming more open to philosophies and theories. The concept of God was not fully grasped; ancient peoples had attempted to convey this during their peak of knowledge. Religion framed God as a man, but in reality, God was much more than that. God is a life-giving energy within the universe. In the times of the Golden Age, visions of grand structures and the use of physics flowed easily into the minds of individuals. Becoming one with the universe fostered a deeper understanding of God—or the perception of God. However, as it stood, the balance of the universe had drifted far from that pinnacle moment, leading to frequent challenges.

Adom expressed that he could help individuals in the Iron Age, as his people maintained a more accurate record of knowledge and history. Though they too were distanced from the Golden Age, they were less affected due to their awareness of this phenomenon. While sharing this knowledge, Adom emphasized that his people were present to guide Earthlings along the proper path and to enhance their newfound awareness through the leaders who would spread this understanding to other scholars and leaders on Earth. He explained that by sharing this wisdom across the universe, he was helping to prevent fear and doubt from entering minds. The universe was more interconnected than many realized; one being's negative actions and thoughts did not stand alone. Just as in a home, every decision impacts those dwelling within its walls.

His words felt as though the hand of God had reached down to speak to them directly. Like prophets of old, with profound insight and abundant evidence, the leaders were eager to share Adom's message across their world.

In the days following this visitation and their return home, Earths' leaders extended invitations for Adom to visit their nations. The aim was to usher Earth into a new era of knowledge and unity, guided by Adom's vast wisdom. This new era required the more prosperous and powerful nations to yield advantages to foster unity and peace among those in "lesser" lands. The vision was a unified planet standing as one world, now aware of the many other worlds that existed. However, this notion was met with skepticism by many on Earth, perceived as foreign at the time. For ages, lands had been defined by their beliefs, whether political or religious, which had solidified their diversity. Divisions and beliefs shaped territories, and if all could share a common belief, there would be one less obstruction to unity. Eventually, if those chains were broken, they would see themselves not only as one world but as one solar system, one galaxy, and ultimately one universe—because that is what they are.

But this was much easier said than done, as we know. Resistance arose; beliefs were often tied to religion, which now faced challenges. In some cases, individuals feared losing their prosperity. Human nature made this task difficult, but a process was in place. Over time, the people began to witness changes—unmistakable signs of progress and advancement. This progress was not only observed among the populace; discussions revealed a tangible sensation of change. The truth is that we are all connected, and when positive energy is present, it becomes almost palpable. Despite persistent skepticism surrounding each step toward progress, true change and benefits would eventually prevail, and humanity would yield to the inevitable.

Advancements continued for some time, with Adom becoming the voice and guide behind this transformation. His role was not perceived as authoritarian; rather, he served as a mentor. The people of Earth sought confirmation that they were proceeding correctly and aligning with the universe's will—what Adom represented. While there was no formal appointment or anointing, they inevitably filtered their actions through Adom's approval and guidance for results to continue. In a subtle way, humanity relinquished some of its autonomy to maintain the positive influence of Adom. As often happens, positive results can lead to complacency among sentient beings.

However, even though most inhabitants seemed content with this new order, some refused to relinquish their ideologies. Minor uprisings occurred, though they were usually met with swift rejection from the masses who found greater self-worth and prosperity. The most significant threats emerged from a geographical area nestled between Greece, Turkey, and Italy. This region, commonly referred to as the Mediterranean, was rife with unrest and discontent. Similar sentiments echoed in the nearby area known as the Middle East, historically referred to as Mesopotamia—a working theory among historians. It was as though this land called to its people, beckoning them to remember days long past. Yet, any real uprisings were quickly suppressed. The leaders, resourced and equipped by Adom and the other Fortunates, managed these outcries without resorting to force or violence. This approach ensured that no one could question the actions and procedures of the new order. They consistently preached that a rise from the Iron Age was beginning.

The Fortunates demonstrated to Earthlings a new way to embrace spiritual and intellectual harmony with the universe. What perplexed many was that in lands that had previously experienced disturbances and rebellion against the Fortunates—like Israel and Palestine—there was now an absence of conflict. The people had begun to accept the ways of the universe while remaining hesitant toward the Fortunates. Overall, there was unprecedented freedom, free from religious wars. This change was attributed to the new knowledge and revelations about history and beliefs that the Fortunates provided. Yet, the undercurrents of rebellion persisted, even if managed. People felt the confusion stemming from a recognition of their differences, prompting even the most zealous adherents of the past to consider new timelines. It raised questions about their long-held religious beliefs that had influenced every action, regardless of consequence. It was as if they had received answers, yet now faced many more questions—though many chose to remain silent. While they desired to fight and protect what was theirs, it was no longer solely for religious reasons embedded in their minds. Instead, they came to believe that war had become a distraction rather than a means of preserving archaic laws. Most remained quiet, even as something deeper called to them. Describing this as the land crying for their help would have sounded almost psychopathic, so they kept those feelings to themselves.

Meanwhile, the Fortunates—particularly Adom and Echo—often reminded the people of Earth that succumbing to the trap of warfare reminiscent of the dark days would engulf Earth and its people for ages. All the new learnings

were designed to preserve life on Earth, granting them eternal abundance. Adom reassured them that they had always been connected to the stars and the universe; humanity only had to allow this understanding to thrive within their beings. They could be saved, but they must be willing to embrace this eternal truth. If they became part of the solution, future generations would benefit from the lessons learned.

Yet, how could they, as humans, come to terms with it? Each individual was pulled toward a truth previously thought lost—

hidden in the void. As mentioned before, they were bound by their beliefs and would only break free when allowed to understand the universe's endless potential. It would take time for humans to appreciate and accept what Adom spoke about and ensure that it resonated deep within their souls.

And so, the stories began to spread from the very heart of it all—an understanding, an acceptance, a union—and slowly but surely, they learned.

By this point, Panspermia had crept just outside Earth's atmosphere. From the surface of Earth, glimpses of the massive orbiting land could be seen at specific moments, often during full moons. They had maintained their orbit for nearly two years, intervening only when they perceived that the Earthlings were hindering their progress toward ascension or upon request.

Yet, throughout the world, the words of Adom were continually reinforced. People became increasingly at peace with themselves and their neighbors. The entire planet was quickly propelled into a more blissful age, all due to the enlightenment of Adom and the other Fortunates who had arrived to save Earth from its darkness—or rather, to accelerate its journey toward the Golden Age. However, it should be noted that harmony is often unattainable without true leadership or authority. Borders remained across the globe, and designations persisted over regions and groups of people. Still, the division and separation that once ran rampant were replaced by a sense of tribal unity.

Eventually, Adom, along with the residents of Panspermia, was offered a place to settle in any region of their choosing. Initially, there was reluctance from Adom, but he soon articulated his reasons for hesitating to occupy Earth. He explained to world leaders that the Fortunates did not wish to disrupt the progress they were experiencing. He feared that the arrival of a different group might undo part of the advancements made among the nations. However, there seemed to be something deeper in his reasoning: the constant reassurance that the people of Earth were making their own decisions. This was his manipulative way of gaining their trust.

Adom always had a plan, and being patient with that plan was one of its most crucial elements. But skepticism grew, and he soon faced challenges as some of Earth's leaders began to voice their concerns vociferously against the reluctance to join the people as equals. Some extreme theories emerged regarding why they would not settle on Earth, suggesting they were performing atmospheric alterations and did not want to plague themselves, or that they were merely waiting for the people of Earth to become more complacent and thus more susceptible to what would inevitably become an attack. Although these theories were unsubstantiated at the time, their prevalence raised concerns, and those wary of the situation began to grow in number.

A consistent behavior among people is that fear can sometimes overshadow rational thought, resulting in irrational actions. This is what those harboring angst about the unfolding events would eventually be told, as the forthcoming actions of the Fortunates would dispel their theories. Before that, however, an uprising began in Rome, particularly in a location known to many of its inhabitants as a sacred area called Vatican City. Perhaps it was because their religion was challenged or their history was jeopardized, but a counterculture was undoubtedly embedding itself. Much of the anger and discontent stemmed from the fact that the savior of mankind was not as prophesied for centuries, but rather an alien from the outer reaches of space, whose origins were unknown to the people. Some accepted that the teachings from the "good book" of law at the center of Vatican City's belief system were merely allegorical or symbolic, lending credence to the idea that Adom and his citizens were what the old authors sought to describe. After all, they would argue, Adom did come in the form of a man, and his arrival had ignited a more peaceful world for them. Yet, there was more at play than just religion, and Adom recognized it. He attributed the unrest not only to their beliefs but also to a challenge of their ethnography.

Nevertheless, this region concentrated most of the discontent and unrest. As we know now, religion and heartfelt beliefs are tough bonds to break. In the end, he is just a man, isn't he?

So, before the questioning grew too loud and before the people could realize there was more to it than religion, Adom catered to the unrest with gradual appeasements. The Tune extracted itself again and found a permanent home at 0:0, the site of the initial meeting place. However, this was quickly met with the same iterations. It was a dome, so atmospheric adjustments would not impact those within the walls of the extracted city. Or, why place it in the middle of the ocean, where it would be difficult for the blue planet to defend itself in case of an attack, implying a quicker, less obstructed escape?

Witnessing the unrest among the planet and the continuous challenges questioning their actions, Adom announced that Panspermia and its inhabitants would accept the invitation to rest the massive vessel in the outer limits of Cairo. Thus, the Fortunates occupied two permanent residences. The upheaval in Vatican City, fueled by underground sects of opposition who suggested that the Fortunates were secretly conducting nefarious acts against the skies of Earth through unrecognized science, was soon dispelled by this move to join the people of Earth. The inevitable consequence of this action, however, would not be nearly as simple as the scrolls of Jacob would one day reveal, as witnessed by the Omniscient One. Others, on a subconscious level, sensed there was a greater story at play, even if they could not articulate it. In some cases, they later explained that it felt almost as if the land itself was calling to them. Unable to explain it, they chose to keep it to themselves, taking comfort in believing it was a religious conviction that motivated them, which was sufficient for their rebellion.

Adom soon challenged all of Earth's leaders to unite and establish a structured government that would facilitate living in unity and prosperity. He explained that on his home planet of Fortuna, a unified government existed, one that fostered a belief in a single planet. This was a crucial step forward in progress for the world. Before this, the lands had continued their previous trades and financial dealings with neighboring regions and regimes, yielding only minor relief, far from the true One World that was needed. Adom pointed out that this was inconsistent with the Fortunates' sermons advocating for a peaceful and harmonious state. Eventually, a neighbor's envy would surface if true equality in a uniform decision-making process was not achieved. Due to the diversity of land and culture worldwide, the people questioned how a deciding government could be implemented. Observing the uneasiness among Earth's populace, Adom challenged them once more, asserting that the answer lay within themselves. There is much to learn from compromise. He would go on to teach. His words would seemingly test their faith and the depth of their belief in what they had learned since "the Summoning."

Suddenly, the framework for this new order appeared to come together effortlessly. A republic would be established, resembling the structured government of the recently established United States. This would grant each country equal power through representation in the republic. The benefits of one land would be shared with others, and while one country might possess greater power due to its landscape, this did not mean that its geography would spell the demise of a nation.

The group settled on a new name: The United Lands of Earth (ULE). At that moment, a profound sense of unification was felt across the globe. Now, more than at any other time since the arrival of the Fortunates, the people of the blue planet sensed that all Adom had spoken of in the past few years was finally coming to fruition. Earth's inhabitants were on the verge of ascension, well ahead of the stars, and in accordance with the foretelling of the Mayan calendar, just as Adom had proclaimed. Their first united decision was to make Adom the president of the U.L.E. With this decision, it is said that Adom smiled.

PAX ROMANA

With persistence and great ingenuity, the people pressed on. The Republic began to take shape. Though the process was inchoate and took time to solidify, it seemed to come together with remarkable ease in the months that followed, leading to nearly a year of full construction. Concerns arose during its formation, as some felt their needs were not being adequately addressed. However, there was no significant animosity worthy of attention; it was as if people needed little reminding that this endeavor was for the greater good.

Once established, the Senate boasted numerous representatives who brought forth questions and concerns on behalf of their constituents. More often than not, discussions centered around the terrain and how to provide adequately for everyone. Many regions lacked an abundance of resources and could not sustain themselves, necessitating continuous shared compromises. All these issues were deliberated within the walls of Panspermia, with essential exposure to the media and the public being willingly offered. A palpable sense of pride enveloped the globe.

Though resistance occasionally reared its combative head, it was only in small pockets. Panspermia, now nestled just north of the Great Pyramid, was imbued with the symbolic might and splendor that the United Lands of Earth (U.L.E.) had to offer.

The U.L.E

The United Lands of Earth was the name given to the new order and republic. A restructuring of Old Earth and its borders was pivotal, particularly in renaming continents and appointing new leaders. The lands are now referred to as follows: "The Nevereaches," representing the northern and southernmost points of Earth; "Epocholia," encompassing most of North America; "Paramatastan," covering Europe, most of western Asia, and the northern tip of Africa; "Syricha," primarily South America; "Labryanthia," comprising mid-Africa and what was previously recognized as Far East Asia; and "Basal," covering the tips of South America, Africa, and all of Australia.

With these renaming's came new leadership, particularly in Paramatastan, which held the most significance. The Fortunates aimed to ensure that their objectives would not be interfered with or opposed to. This also served to further disassociate the people of Earth from their history. New names symbolize new beginnings, eventually leading to a deterioration of the bonds people felt with their land. However, this did not occur in the region of the Vatican, where the people in close proximity would come to be known as Acre. The ties that bind was stronger here, likely due to deep-seated sentiments, but it cannot be overlooked that the majority of the population had fallen victim to the Fortunates' persuasive influence, enabling them to achieve their aims.

Ocean
Epocholia
Pacific
Ocean
Atlantic
Ocean
Syricha

Arctic
Ocean
...ches North
...ramatastan
...ke
Labryanthia
Basal
Pacific
Ocean
...es South

While business was conducted inside Panspermia, the external atmosphere was equally captivating. Every day, the Endicots lined up outside, creating a path toward the grand capital's entrance. It was truly a sight to behold, with hundreds arriving daily just to witness the spectacle. Officials entered and exited freely, reinforcing the sense of transparency and accessibility.

Over time, a city formed around Panspermia. Residential structures were built to accommodate chambers and dwellings, and where there were living spaces, commercial buildings and merchants soon followed. In the eyes of the Earthlings, Panspermia quickly became the shining beacon of success and prosperity for the rest of the world. Its massive footprint and sprawling presence evoked a sense of inherent authority, leading the Earthlings to fall in line naturally. However, some voices occasionally rose, claiming that this had all happened before. They questioned whether these echoes were merely metaphorical comparisons to great empires of the past or if they truly believed that history was repeating itself. Regardless, the masses moved forward, granting only a fleeting moment of attention to these concerns as they pressed onward, their eyes fixed upward.

Governments were established throughout the land, with officials elected as representatives for each nation. Civil discourse and debate were facilitated thoughtfully and carefully, helping to form procedures and laws for the world's residents. In-fighting was foreign, and respect abounded—this, of course, was largely due to the authority of Panspermia. While some recognized the land of Old Earth, still known as Egypt, most accepted that the capital of the world had now shifted to Panspermia.

Once elected, government officials were held in high regard, yet they were also kept grounded and approachable by their constituents. The balance of power remained stable, and equity was carefully monitored. Sensible and clear laws were enacted to govern the Republic's people, with none contested due to their apparent fairness—especially given how Adom presented them. The initial wave of regulation was subtle yet necessary, encompassing mandates like required schooling and financial governance. The concepts of karma, universal balance, and the positioning of the stars became central tenets of education, alongside an edification that spread throughout society. Through this framework, all other elements would fall into place—a teaching that continues to this day.

One of the great lessons imparted by the Fortunates was that all energy in the universe is interconnected. The source of energy within each being, the soul, remains part of the greater energy from which it originated. When religions previously taught that God lives within us, they were not wrong; it was simply a different way of explaining the same truth. The form of government was also maintained, albeit on a smaller scale due to environmental factors. Throughout the Republic, all rules were uniform, allowing no room for interpretation or regional adjustment. Even the clocks were standardized, with all time beginning in the city of Panspermia.

Essentially, the sun rose for a new day in Panspermia, and the calendar was reset to December 21, 2012, recognized as Date 0. From this point, it was marked as Ascension Day, Year One, moving forward. This reset led to confusion surrounding calendars. The old Julian calendar also used the acronym AD, beginning at the time of the Savior's death and documenting the day he rose again, as referred to in Jacob's Scrolls. While history was taught, the emphasis on personal memory gained strength. It was instilled that history is merely a retelling of a story, but it could become so much more if absorbed as memory. Within a memory lies the truth. We were taught that this had happened before, that stories could be just that. By absorbing history as memory, people allowed themselves to lose their path, becoming vulnerable to others telling their story and, ultimately, taking advantage of them.

Though harmony and inclusion prevailed over any one belief or religion, the narrative was still being told by others, a situation that must never be repeated. During this period of peaceful pursuit, it is said that religion was neither completely dissolved nor forbidden; rather, a focus on positive outcomes and equity for all superseded the fractures and divisions often propagated by religion. Above all, a powerful sense of faith in the Republic united people beyond their individual beliefs and practices.

Time was determined on a twenty-four-hour rotation in accordance with Earth. The calendar was based on ancient pre-Panspermia records collected by Julian's scribes. As previously stated, the new starting date was established as December 22, shortly before the arrival of the Fortunates. The year was adjusted from "2012" to a new indicator: 0 A.D. (which stood for Ascension Day but took on a new meaning). Now it represented Earth and the universe, leading to a duality in the abbreviated acronym AD. If the old calendar was referenced, it was understood that the 2012 revolutions of Earth had been added. While the new calendar was widely accepted and followed under Panspermia's authority, groups found in and around the Mediterranean clung to their old records.

They remained loyal to their calendar, which was based on their religion's Savior, including his arrival date and death. Other religions also adhered to their timelines in various locations, but the Vatican remained particularly adamant and unwavering in its commitment to the past. It was as if they were driven by an endogenous feeling, a recognizable voice within them. Their adherence to the past was not merely a matter of tradition; it seemed as though a memory was embedded within their minds. Although initial discussions on the topic were often avoided, these memories called out to them after days of events, prompting them to hold tightly to their heritage. While this was frowned upon throughout the world, the general sentiment was that this reluctance signified a failure to adopt the new way. An easier explanation was to blame their faith in religion, though it was much deeper than that.

The Vatican's reluctance to embrace Panspermia's changes signaled a small form of rebellion by holding onto their ancient calendars. Nevertheless, most customs were still observed, and even the new world calendar was utilized when the Vatican engaged with more sensitive audiences. This defiance and inconsistency posed challenges to the early record-keeping of this age. Due to confusion around dates, and in many cases a lack thereof, we are compelled to reference both calendars found in the "Scrolls of Jacob."

And so, the Republic thrust forward.
These educational mandates were among the most significant adjustments for the Earthlings. Now, instead of what was known as core subjects of old, it was the study of the stars and universe that mattered most, for it was these subjects that the Fortunates spoke of on the day of the first meeting with world leaders. An example of new teachings was the revelation that the "Golden Age" of humanity had arrived thousands of years earlier than expected due to the Fortunates' arrival. Even though the balance of the universe was still yet to be aligned, the knowledge of one's past and recognition of its history was part of the strain that would engulf one's way of thinking and allow you to fall victim to the universe not yet being in line. It is a battle within one's mind daily when you are engulfed in the Iron Age. Yes, it is a challenge to maintain the mind during the process of being mired in the Iron Age, but progress can still be made during this period; it is just more cumbersome. While structures, inventions, and philosophical

thinking are more attainable during the Golden Age, as we have been told that the might and power of the mind made the famed Pyramids of northern Egypt of Old Earth simplified and came with great ease, still many great things can happen during the periods of Declension or moving forward during the Ascension. With this, the knowledge of one's history was constantly reinforced and became that much more important. In their history lie truths. Even if the past is not what we would want to embrace, it is with the past that we can recognize our faults and secure our actions from repeating them. Although education was mandatory among the young, adults were encouraged to learn the new curriculum. While you can't truly move space and time, what you can do is contemplate how they are impacting what and how you think.

In other teachings, there was philosophy and theoretical thinking. With this, the brain was exercised, and equational math was initiated but geared towards engineering and creating new science and physics. The stress and significant learnings would constantly be of history. It was now seen in a whole new way. That didn't mean that historical references didn't happen. They were just taught that it happened for different reasons. The past was challenged more. But when there was a challenge to the timeline, most notably the 26,000-year clock, silence was encouraged, almost as though the Fortunates were reluctant to tell history from its true beginnings. Another always engaging question was how the Fortunates knew so much about Earth's history, but just as quickly as the question was raised, so too was the disbursement of it.

The chambers would proceed with injunctions and requests from the governing body–continuing with what appeared to be "normal" functions. Certain minor conflicts and debates occurred amongst most lands, but for the most part, they were resolved and dispersed rather quickly and with complete civility. They would see more times than Adom intervening on these issues. He offered such a superior form of etiquette and grace–and what appeared to be pure logic and empathy–that any nation that did bring forth an issue would reach a satisfactory resolution promptly–and the issue itself would dissolve without question. Just as one of the more significant ones, that being the dissolving process of nuclear weapons. This aspect was tempered with great caution, but with Adom's encouragement or rather confirmation, as the gesture was not brought forward by the Fortunates, but by the smaller countries. Some still think it is possible that Adom or Echo had initiated the idea, but the trail of conversation was lost and ended at the point of others. And Adom did support the mandate while always saying that their very presence was an act of war, even when lying dormant.

But governing such a vast collection of lands and people–including balancing their multiple issues and preferences–proved time-consuming for Adom. Though he appeared truly concerned with the opinions that people held dear, in reality, he recognized these simple issues as more of a shackle on the progress of Earthlings. One that was holding them back from true potential. He knew there were greater, more universal decisions that should be prioritized to move the world toward his ultimate goal for them. Or at least that is how he projected it. As we now know, it kept him from his potential and timeline.

So, in what would be recognized as a first-of-its-kind "executive order" made by Adom, the contract for the "Six Continents" was created. The lands moving forward would be known as Epocholia, Paramatastan, Labyrinthia, Syarich, Basal, and the Nevereaches North and South. The treaty limited its routine interactions to only six leaders instead of the unruly and often impossible number of one hundred and ninety-five. According to Adom, there were many benefits to this decision.

Firstly, the six continents would individually have more knowledge of one's geographical complications due to their familiarity and proximity to each land mass. But what sold the Earthlings on this radical change was the implication that he would be placing more responsibility on Earthlings themselves. This prospect of personal liberty propped up their confidence and self-sufficiency and played to the inherent value of freedom they all seemed to crave.

While it was a bit complex, it evolved rapidly. It may have been due to imitating the already recognized Roman Republic, but what it also allowed for was an unrecognized manipulation. Nowhere was this done more than in the land of Paramatastan, where a younger candidate than others was rising in popularity: Magnus Carter was placed as the land's representative. Of course, he was not just anointed the position; there would be a vote amongst the people. That was the way of the Fortunates, always making everything appear as though they were making a choice. So, in the days leading up to a vote, not just in Paramatastan but all of the other lands of the U.L.E., attention was not focused on just one campaign, and the people of the world were unaware of what was occurring, or if they were, they were all just too consumed with all other happenings.

It was done by constant support from the media, which seemed to always show Magnus in a good light or at times just simple glitches during challengers' campaigns like a power failure or a service disruption during one's speech. Unfortunately, this was only recognized or rather exposed in later days and would not be given much thought or attention by the masses. Maybe even more so because the media placed emphasis on the surprising vote that occurred in Basal. The region was mainly the geographical location of the continent of Australia, but due to its incorporation of some of the Far East Asian collection, an Asian leader rose through the ranks and seized victory. There was not much discernment from the Australian community, but the media seemed to have forcibly made it a story, and with that, much less attention was paid to the Magnus campaign and ultimately his victory. As always, people move on, and what may have only been thought of as conspiracy theories at the time of the incidents, by the time it is exposed and confirmed as fact, it would at that point only be a footnote. And Magnus was already entrenched in the Republic and eventually absorbed in the governing body that he was

almost unrecognized, and most didn't care until it was much too late. Inauspiciously, many felt they heard Adom give way and refer to the man as Magna occasionally, but the common ear thought it to be just a mishap, and in many scenarios, he was occasionally referred to as both Magnus and Magna.

Once appointed as leaders over their new lands, Adom requested that they govern as he had, with compassion and care. He implored them to look within the soul and wait for that feeling when the universe provides guidance. He would tell them to "be one" with the universe and let it, in turn, become one with them.

In the meantime, peace and self-awareness framed the message behind this order of realignment and the new government, so much so that once fully presented, citizens of each newly apportioned land embraced it almost hypnotically.

Once adopted, the house of Panspermia took advantage of this free time to continue embedding and pushing forward greater learning, knowledge, and prosperity. To the citizens of Earth, it was a wonderful trade-off. They would create mandates and prioritize them.

Adom was not a president at all. He had evolved without notice into an Emperor. And due to the peace and prosperity of all the people, it was accepted. And it was seen as though the people had chosen this way and in turn chosen him.

And any discourse or challenge to the newly constructed lands, as those that did oppose it would constantly point out that their history was being lost and even greater opposition would state that it was being done with intent. But again, it cannot be stressed anymore that when people are in a state of peace and prosperity, they will tend to disparage any voice of concern and blissfully follow along with one's mandates and laws.

One notable example of an important Panspermia priority was that of the eco-pods. These differed from the 0-0 model, known as the Tune, which landed on the day of the Summoning and had now taken up permanent residency at this location. Instead, these new models were not constructed previously, and the people of Earth did not know how to achieve the scientific knowledge to create a massive dome without collapsing. It was said to have been a challenge for ages of physicists. While the engineering was not truly known, the individual parts of the new construct were, and with a sort of assembly line, would be encouraged. This may have been done with the intent that the overall recipe for creating this new marvel was withheld purposefully. That was consistent with all of the technology presented by the Fortunates. So, while Earthlings were exposed to the creations and felt they were part of it, in reality, they were sheltered from the true completion. It cannot be stated more than already done that everything was done with precision and intent.

But construction continued without the acknowledgment of what was occurring, and when placed together, it was no larger than a half-meter high and two meters wide and had the appearance of a case or box. It was then placed in its location of agreed-upon choice, exactly one meter below the Earth's surface, across the planet. When activated, it would build a biosphere of even greater magnitude than Earth had witnessed. Utilizing micro-biotics that could regenerate autonomously, they would build a hexagonal-shaped pyramid with dimensions nearly 440 meters from its center. The material used would filter the current atmosphere and remove unnecessary toxins or poisons from the air. It would continue to then build structures within itself. Immediately, this new technology resolved what concerned most Earthlings at that time–the fear that their atmosphere was deteriorating.

What they did not know at the time was that this particular science would be used to advance Earthlings' greater explorations that lay ahead. This, of course, was the real reason behind the Fortunates' gift to Earth, but the immediate satisfaction was welcomed. The design itself was intentional. The walls at the base were nearly 10 meters high and then peaked towards its pyramidical zenith. As we all know, a hexagon shape is superior at maximizing space. Due to a flat-edged design, the walls of two hexagon-shaped Eco pods can be placed next to one another, allowing for easy entry from one to another and no need for any sort of bridge or tunnel from one structure to the next. This was important, as the original eco-pod that the Earthlings witnessed was dome-shaped and lacked many of these important qualities. But those were needed for travel, and these Eco pods were needed for stability and settling.

Hive City became one of the first locations where these massive Eco pods were introduced. Placed near the southernmost point of the Nevereaches North, in what was previously known as Siberia, the powerful design and technology behind the Eco-Pods gave way to livable conditions. This land, previously considered uninhabitable (as was most of the Nevereaches North and South), was provided an urban stamp of civilization with now hyperborean. This would also give lands equal possibility that were less fortunate due to their geographical limitations.

While Earthlings were later taught how to construct, they lacked the physical material, and the Fortunates only provided this. Beyond just lands and creation, another power came to be due to Eco-pods: Regen. The Eco pods would become incredibly important to the advancements of the Earthlings, and even to this day, science is still regarded as a wonder of its time.

Regen, a powerful form of teleportation, would become more significant as time passed and would be very important in the coming uprisings. It was introduced to Earthlings at the time to make occupying the Eco-Pods simpler. However, the science of this marvel was not quite available to the Earthlings based on their limitations and levels of intellect. Adom, and the rest of the Fortunates, would choose to abstain from sharing that technology until the time was right, he said, but it was later understood that it was merely a cloning of the cells rather than teleporting them. The original embodiment would dissolve, and the entity that once was no longer existed. All of the DNA was transferred, even the memories of oneself. The introduction was performed in masse. The science behind it was not offered to the people, for it would have received moral backlash as the person in its newly found location was truly a clone, even though it was now the only being to exist as the original cells deteriorated. This was used to populate Hive City so that physically reaching the Nevereaches would prove an arduous journey had it been performed without Regen. Within an Eco pod would be Regen hubs so that once an Eco Pod was created, it was easily accessed from another.

The beginnings of the Republic and its progress were rapid, blissful, and somewhat euphoric for the Earthlings. Mesmerized by the splendor of it all, there was no way to suspect Panspermia's greater plan for them. Like an underground stream rushing beneath lush meadows, a more clandestine purpose rooted in every decision that Adom and the Fortunates made. The blood of Earthlings was predominant in the design of this plan. It would be their blood that was requested in the end. And it would be requested from every last one of them.

<u>Hive City</u>

Located in the Nevereaches North (Siberia of Old Earth), a collection of Eco-Pods was placed together to create the first established livable area on Earth in what was once thought of as an uninhabitable location. This was intentionally done to showcase the advantages of such technology. It would bring equality to locations that had unfortunate geographical hardships. Hive City would become famous due to it being the greatest collection, seven in all, of Eco-Pods, and a once undesirable area had now become a destination requested by some to relocate or just visit. The challenges of living in such a region were minimized, and with that, the goal of populating all areas of Earth was equally dispensed.

A Regen station was constructed in every Eco-Pod throughout the world to make traveling to and from easier, especially to destinations such as Hive City in Siberia. The science and awareness of the challenges were greatly appreciated by those of Earth, and that was always the goal of the Fortunates. Having the Earthlings accept and embrace the technology, and their consideration of the people was for comfort and peace throughout their occupation so that their motives were not questioned and they could pursue their ultimate goal. It would also be an easier transition for the pure ones that would later be selected to come with them and occupy Ecopolis.

Over time, once again, skepticism and questioning arose throughout the lands. The citizens of Earth became distrusting people after a while. While world unity and peace were definitely at their highest levels in history, the uprisings, documented in the historical notes of Peter and then transcribed in the "Scrolls of Jacob" never ceased. And though they were often silenced, there was one, we are told, that held significance: an uprising from the region known as Crete.

This uprising became so organized and powerful that it required the intervention of one of the most famous Endicots to live as the world was *introduced to Ajax. It was almost too organized, though. The accounts often contradicted each other. Some mention that no bloodshed occurred, while others state there was plenty. It was the accounts of bloodshed within the uprising that is said to have become the rebellion's undoing. In the end, every last citizen was accounted for. As the world watched, the Fortunates leveraged intellect and diplomacy in defusing the matter, and the harshest force used was the simple detainment of the agitators. Because they refused to spread lies about a violent Panspermia, these individuals were branded as conspiracy theorists, enemies of the state, and, at worst, terrorists.*

Throughout the world, a sentiment was adopted that the Vatican was at the seat of rebellion, and many began turning on the Christian faith. Let it also be known that Crete was where the seated Pope at the time had hailed from.

Peter's question was simple, yet it echoed loudly: 'Why?' He made sure it was impossible to ignore. This region, loyal to the Pope, may have had a small population, but it was home to many of his closest family and friends. Peter's relentless repetition of that question sparked a firestorm, catapulting him to notoriety. Thus was born one of the most powerful voices of the time—Peter Deluca, who would become both hero and villain in equal measure

Peter DeLuca

Born in the southern part of Italy was a man named Peter DeLuca. He grew up to be a hard, rugged man with firm principles, but there was always a heart behind his principles. At a young age, he moved with his parents to NYC. His straightforwardness may sometimes have been misconstrued and appeared argumentative, but it was always for wanting to seek and do the right thing.

Above all else, his character was inquisitive, which may have been for the protection of those he loved. Or maybe it was something deeper seeded in his mind, and he wasn't aware it was a question from within. He was always trying to figure out who he was. And when significant occurrences in the world would happen, like those on monumental days, Peter DeLuca would begin to question everything. And like so many others born in the Mediterranean region, he felt a calling to this area. So, for others that had always lived there and felt an inner calling, for Peter it was different; he needed to uproot his family and return to the region where he was born.

He asked such thought-provoking questions during this time that people began to follow him. He wasn't driven by religion, though the government would convince others he was. No, for Peter, it was just the question, "Why?" It was for his own historical understanding. And while it may have been right what he was doing, it was frowned upon by the masses due to strong government and media persuasion, but as long as he felt he was justified for being a free thinker, that was all that mattered to him.

He continued to believe that the Fortunates were intentionally or at least eclectically distorting history, and history should be told in full or not told at all, so thought Peter. And no matter the challenges, Peter would get to the bottom. For that was who he was.

During the unsettling times, which mostly occurred in the region of the Vatican, those around the world were less combative and more accepting of the Fortunates. Most of the world was seeing and feeling a sense of euphoria as their enlightenment and riches were gaining every day. This was even seen within the region of the Mediterranean, but the people there or who would migrate there had a different perception of their gains and were drawn to feeling compelled to question every move of the Fortunates. It was deeply ingrained in their souls that the Fortunates were doing things for their own progress or, worse, had nefarious intentions. That was no different for Peter.

As his voice had gained a following, it also grabbed the attention of the Fortunates, and their intent was to have this man seen as an enemy. Not just to the Fortunates but to the progression of the people of Earth. It began to become easier for the Fortunates to align him with being more than just an adversary in speech, but an actual threat to the Republic as little by little his attire went from that of just a police officer from the streets of New York to a soldier as he increased his visible arms of guns being outwardly exposed for all to see. But the people of Earth were not given the story as for why he increased his defending armory. He was a threat to the progress and plan of the Fortunates and therefore needed to protect his family, friends, and himself at all times. And so, the police officer of NYC was now a soldier of the Infidels.

TAMING THE REBELLION

Accounts tell us that Peter Deluca was a simple man, though his figure was imposing. Often found in his worn combat boots and rugged attire, he was always ready for combat, but nothing insinuated that he would initiate or go about his business in such a manner.

Records indicate that physical conflict was rare at first, but Peter knew the time would come for action if things continued this way, and he wasn't one to be caught off guard. His build was muscular, and his face was worn with stress. He was a solid character, not one to react irrationally or respond out of terms. His ultimate priority was peacekeeping amongst the questioners and division amongst the Fortunates. He just wanted answers that would make more sense.

While others would question the actions of the Fortunates, it wouldn't be long before they would somewhat forget or not continue forging ahead. It may have been due to them providing for their families or maybe just complacency that would have overtaken their fight. It is a tough character trait to maintain every day. It is a dutiful purpose to wake up questioning every day, that can eventually wear a person down, making it easier to accept. Peter was not that person, though.

Eventually, his name caught the eyes and ears of Adom regularly, and Adom was going to see to it that this individual would need to be dealt with. It was a constant reminder that the people within the Panspermia walls would hear the name every day, and Adom was the one that would do it. It was a cunning task, but unlike others that would come and go, Adom recognized him and would constantly slip into the people's minds. He wouldn't say it with angst or hatred,

that would have been out of character for Adom, but it would be more subliminal. He would approach his name with either a smile or, in other cases, a verisimilitude concern for the man.

That is what reports came back as saying, but he did start to encourage people to notice and, more importantly, recognize him as an impediment to the people's progress. With an encouragement that would have him in a way of asking to sort of tie him to the Vatican. He was said to have asked other officials, "Does he have ties to the Vatican?" constantly and almost in the same breath, "Oh yes, that's right, you had said no," and then would gasp, almost blaming himself for being so forgetful. But say things enough and even a question can start becoming a truth. Adom was very adroit in this manner.

Tying him to the Vatican would become a difficult task, though. Peter had no bonded ties to the Christian faith aside from him maintaining the traditions that would come along with his upbringing. The only thing he had in common with the Vatican was that they all were skeptical of their new guests. It was this common ground only that would align with the thoughts of others. He did not take up residency behind the walls of the Vatican, nor was he often seen on the grounds at the time, if at all, but the Fortunates were trying to make that assertion. They wanted to make it seem that there was only one group to target instead of multiple pockets sprouting.

The only thing that did make it at all easy to do was the proximity of Peter's new residency since returning to Italy. Though it was outside the walls of the Vatican, he still resided somewhat nearby. And the question was raised as to why he would travel from New York City back to this region. But Peter would tell us later in the Scrolls that it was a calling that he had but could not explain. The masses were not privy to that message until much later on.

As the Republic continued to sink its talons into the minds of the United Lands of Earth's (ULE) citizens, Peter and his band of followers, and maybe it was because of the constant referencing of the Vatican that Peter would draw an alliance with the church-state. They both held onto their suspicions of Adom and the Fortunates, and numbers began to multiply somewhat secretively. And just like a phrase that holds true through years before and years to come, *in unity there is strength*, and though their true beliefs may not have been the basis for their contentiousness towards the visitors, they did have a centro-lineal mind. And their hold at the Vatican would seem more presentable and uninformed.

With every major proposal or mandate issued by Panspermia, there was a swift and expected push back from the opposition. The traditionalists would launch counter initiatives almost machine-like throughout their many chapters in the ULE, cautioning Earthlings to pay attention to the underlying purposes of Panspermia's *adjustments*. Though most ignored them, numbers were added at a steady click to the Vatican's membership, and Peter's influence eventually could no longer be subtly ignored by the Fortunates.

With a growing presence of contention, Adom sought to ramp up pressure to silence the rebellion. The task wasn't nearly as simple as one may suggest. Though an undying devotion to Panspermia had become rampant throughout the land, the Earthlings were known to balk at attempts to silence push back. This was a unique trait within their physiology. Concepts like freedom and liberty were still quite important to them, even if they had subconsciously forsaken many of their liberties in exchange for the profound peace that Adom had provided. Therefore, effectively silencing those with what they would sometimes publicly refer to as heterodox beliefs had to be carefully balanced between a swift view of force and a soft embrace of "free thought."

The imposing and intimidating Endicots were often leveraged for such a task. The soldiers, however, were built as blind, fiercely loyal servants to Adom and his leadership. This often caused a more abrasive approach to handling rebels. It was also recognized as the alien race policing and enforcing its will on the host. Though there are numerous accounts of bloodshed and cold-blooded violence at the hands of the Endicots, the soothsaying journalists and media controllers of Panspermia worked overtime to paint a more victimized picture. Often, whenever members of the Vatican-led counter efforts were violently killed or maimed, the messaging from Adom's leadership painted stories of self-defense and brutal behavior on behalf of the rebels. In many cases, due to the talented ability of Adom and the Fortunates to explain situations to the Earthlings, the death of rebels became

a cause for celebration. The constant reinforcement of words that Adom had used to describe such people would be something like ascension detractors, enlightenment clouds, and progress resistors.

To drive this negative messaging further into the public rhetoric, the Panspermia-controlled media soon began referring to members of Peter's cause as "Infidels." This was a perfect description, they would say, of the types of people who choose "lies over truth" and attempt to attack a more perfect union. It was a familiar term in the religious sects of old. Most people had an almost innate negative reaction to the phrase, and, for most of the ULE, it became a common household phrase.

At this time, Peter began to transcribe all incidents on paper and thus would eventually become known to us as *The Scrolls of Jacob*, his son initiated. None knew of these writings, and Peter kept them all in a vault. He realized then that history would not be recalled accurately if he allowed the ULE to write it. Placing it on paper and delivering it to the masses was not as conducive or even productive in the sense of delivering, but it was the only thing he trusted now. He probably didn't even see at the time that they would be dispensed, for years later, his son Jacob transcribed them as scrolls. Trust is essential in a time of unrest and questioning. It is not as though he thought there were spies amongst them, but you can never be too sure what a person will do when under duress, so they were kept to himself. Luckily for us, an account of history would not have been able to be told otherwise.

Peter and the other Vatican followers soon began to own the identifier. With time, the Infidels grew more organized and structured. Because of this, the rebellion grew more frequent and damaging. Adom soon realized that between the struggles of the Endicot's abrasive approach, and the gaining popularity of the Infidels' martyrdom, a new plan to control the rebellion was needed. The first step he took was the creation of "Legions" amongst this ULE. This broke each unique land into two parts–or Legions–to allow for more manageable governance over criminal activity and day-to-day control. Serving as a form of guard or army, the 12 legions were separately governed within each land, reporting directly to the leader of that land and the Fortunates. In addition, a 13th Legion was established.

The 13th Legion

In response to growing unrest and the perception of overly aggressive enforcement by the Endicots, Adom instituted a new system of control. Two legions of highly skilled soldiers were deployed to each new land, forming a total of 12 legions. This move was prompted by widespread concern, even among those not aligned with the opposition, about the heavy-handed tactics used to quell uprisings.

The situation was further complicated by the unease many Earth residents felt about being policed by extraterrestrial visitors. Adom recognized that this growing discontent could threaten the peace between Fortunates and Earthlings. As opposition mounted, the state began to resemble a police state controlled by aliens. In response, anyone branded as a free thinker was strategically labeled an "Infidel," regardless of their ties to the Vatican.

Recognizing the potential for revolution, Adom knew more drastic measures were necessary. The committee swiftly established the Legions. Although historically legions consisted of larger numbers, the term was still recognized as representing enforcers and warriors. While most of the legions were composed of a centurion of soldiers, the 13th Legion was different.

The 13th Legion was designed to be more than just soldiers and enforcers against the opposition; they were to be the elite of the elite. Promoted as the saving grace for all humankind, their mission was to abolish the Infidels once and for all.

Members of the 13th Legion were not just highly skilled soldiers from various ranks and military divisions; they were the best of their kind. Many came from special task forces that had carried out the most elite operations for their respective lands. While they hailed from all over the world, a significant portion came from the Old Earth United States.

The selection process for the 13th Legion was rigorous and specific, considering not only their skills but also how well their speech and image would be projected to the public. Committees and review boards were established to ensure everything was all right and would be accepted by the public. These soldiers were to become the new heroes of the people.

NEWS
77
13
13
ULE
NEWS

Through media manipulation, these soldiers were promoted as stars among men. They were constantly in the public eye, appearing before, during, and after battles. They made appearances in commercials and cameos on shows and events. Their message consistently reinforced that the Infidels were holding back extraordinary achievements for the world.

The 13th Legion became living, breathing gods among men. Unlike the alien Endicots, when these human soldiers used force, it was accepted by the public. Adom's plan had worked to perfection, creating a buffer between the alien rulers and the human population, effectively quelling dissent while maintaining control.

This elite group consisted of 13 highly trained human soldiers, forming a unit dedicated to special operations warfare. Their primary mission was to respond to any form of rebellion, with the Infidels as their main target. Quickly heralded as a team of superhuman heroes, they were elevated among Earthlings and given an aura of immortality. Though entirely mortal, the media leveraged their combat and strategic skills for various purposes, from entertainment to propaganda.

The 13th Legion was marketed to the public as stars among men, from their appearance to their speech. Their careful selection based on both skills and public appeal paid off, as Adom had hoped. The public readily accepted them, making it easier to suppress rebellion. Any aggressive handling of the "Infidels" was now tolerated, as these were their own people, unlike the alien Endicots policing them before.

Regen technology was often used to deploy the legions into battle, giving the impression that they were omnipresent. The true nature of Regen was unknown, and the soldiers genuinely believed they were teleporting. It remains uncertain whether they would have accepted this technology had they known its true nature.

Media outlets frequently broadcasted small battles and highly publicized victories over the Infidels. Regular updates and reassurances from

Panspermia to the citizens of ULE became commonplace. Despite these efforts, the "threat" of the so-called terrorist organization was kept at bay, reduced to a topic of casual conversation at dinner tables and family gatherings. However, beneath the veil of propaganda surrounding the 13th Legion and the Vatican, more believers in ancient religious texts and critics of the new Panspermia regime found refuge in the Infidel stronghold.

The Infidels eventually learned the locations of the regen ports scattered throughout the world for easy accessibility. They used this knowledge to their advantage, either preparing for the Legions' arrival or staging their protests and targeting areas where they knew the Legions wouldn't be present. This strategy allowed the Infidels to maintain their fight and spread their message.

Life continued at this pace for what seemed like a decade. The exact timeline is unclear due to the existence of two calendars, and even Peter's writings can be challenged for accuracy. However, the chronology has little impact on the events themselves. The Fortunates continued to issue small, inconspicuous mandates and regulations while the citizens of ULE basked in the glow of a unified humanity. Although most mandates faced pushback and public disdain from Peter and the Infidels, the situation appeared stable. That is, until Adom issued a bewildering requirement that caught the world off guard.

Panspermia subtly *suggested* that all Earthlings be required to provide a blood sample to the high government. While there had been similar demands for censuses and registries, this was the first time humans were asked to provide such a sensitive, organic part of their identity for registration. Pushback began to build, fueled heavily by the Infidels. The six nation leaders were soon inundated with questions and concerns. Even some officials viewed it as a gross overstepping of people's rights.

In a masterful display, Adom emerged from Panspermia's towers to address humanity. His explanation was met with an overwhelmingly positive response. The decision to collect blood samples, they claimed, was to develop life-saving medical interventions and disease control measures. They also promised to introduce similar organic technology from Panspermia to Earth, potentially increasing the lifespan of

Earthlings. These two issues had long plagued humanity before Adom's arrival, and now a solution seemed within reach. Given the Fortunates' proven track record of innovation in infrastructure and climate control, there was little doubt they could deliver on these more personal concerns.

History shows that the desire to provide blood samples became nearly universal after Adom's explanation. Millions of Earthlings dutifully lined up to support his efforts. However, as usual, the Vatican's opposition echoed through the chambers of the six nations. The Scrolls of Jacob record that the Fortunates' demand for blood provided new fuel for the Infidels'. Their message of sinister intentions by the Fortunates gained some validity. Previously, many of their arguments had been less alarming. Instead of life-threatening warnings about Adom's mandates, the Infidels had shared milder concerns with Earthlings, such as fears of property loss or a gradual erosion of personal liberty. But now, with the demand for blood, Peter and his leaders' voices grew louder. Rebellion gained a firm foothold, and thousands of Earthlings began to openly question their leaders.

Although Adom's explanation satisfied the majority, he feared the power of this new wave of rebellion. In response, he deployed the 13th Legion along with two other legions in a covert, full-force attack on the Vatican. A total of 213 soldiers, led by Luther Carter (brother of Magnus Carter), were tasked with the operation. Luther's involvement intrigued the Vatican, as Magnus was the ULE's representative of Paramatastan, which occupied most of old Europe.

The attack began at twilight on the third day of the week and continued for nearly two days. While the heavily sheltered Vatican kept most citizens of Rome and surrounding areas from witnessing the gruesome details, the Scrolls describe the fighting between the Legions and those that occupied the walled city as intense. Although specific casualty numbers are not provided, the Scrolls suggest nearly fifty Infidels were killed, with only a few Legionnaires suffering minor injuries. Even the Pope was slain, reportedly by the captain of the 13th Legion himself, Aaron Moore, who later denied all accounts. Eyewitness reports claim the Pope approached the captain calling for a truce, but Moore allegedly stabbed him at close range.

The Legionaries, trained soldiers, faced mostly unarmed, concerned citizens. The attack was coordinated and precise. To the outside world, the battles were reported as heated arguments behind Vatican walls. Luther was presented to the public not as a general, but as a government representative appointed by Magnus. The 13th Legion secretly disposed of the Infidels' bodies to maintain the illusion of peace.

Peter, along with the remaining Infidels who survived the conflict, knew the truth but agreed to present a less threatening message to the public. The Pope's death was attributed to his age and the toll of heated discussions.

With no central figure to pass final judgment on their actions, the Infidels were left in disarray. Some outsiders believed this would help progress and quell division, assuming it was primarily the older generation clinging to past beliefs. While exposing the violent response could have damaged the Fortunates' reputation – a key victory for the Infidels – the resulting division and panic would have set back the efforts of both the Vatican and Panspermia.

There was no attempt to ignite a war, as such efforts would have been futile given the Fortunates' superior technology. Peter opposed the group's decision to remain silent but understood the reasoning. While Earth had made great technological strides with the Fortunates' help, it was widely believed that the Fortunates withheld certain truths about their technology. This perception was reality, as Adom carefully controlled what knowledge was released to prevent it from being used against him.

The Fortunates always had a plan, always maneuvering strategically. Even the attack itself was carried out by fellow Earthlings. A full-scale war would likely have ended the human race, especially since Adom's divisive tactics meant Earth wouldn't have been unified against their "guests." Peter had witnessed too many instances where events he thought would open people's eyes were ignored or easily manipulated, making further effort seem futile.

The scrolls describe in detail how Peter begrudgingly agreed to the cover-up. It sickened him, but he knew there would be a better time and place to act. This event solidified Peter's and others' understanding that their newly found "friends" were not what they seemed. They realized they were living under an occupation and surviving it would require immense effort and patience.

It took only weeks for the dust to settle and for Earthlings to move on from the incident. By this time, Panspermia had become experts at controlling media output. Negative events received brief coverage before being quickly replaced with additional propaganda, diverting citizens' attention. While some groups managed to keep old issues alive, most were funded by the resistance, which automatically diminished their credibility.

The Fortunates expertly pitted neighbor against neighbor when needed, countering propaganda with more propaganda. They used celebrations to mask unfortunate events, maintaining a positive atmosphere among the people. Soon, information became the enemy, and Panspermia was seen as the savior. Human nature's inclination to believe in a better future worked in their favor, while the Infidels' constant negativity pushed people away.

THE VATICAN'S SEARCH FOR TRUTH

In the weeks following the Legion's attacks, Peter closed the walls of the Vatican to provide rest and healing for all within. During this time, little was heard from him or the Infidels. Many believed this silence signaled the end of the Vatican's attempts to undermine Adom. In reality, as recorded in the Scrolls, it marked the beginning of a new chapter. From that day forward, many referred to it as Fort Vatican.

During this period of apparent quiet, Peter's main advisors uncovered crucial intelligence from deep within Panspermia, revealing more sinister motives behind the recent demand for Earthling blood samples. This information, supplied by a spy near Ancient Cairo, was groundbreaking. For years, the Infidels had relied on hunches and trends, but now they had concrete evidence.

The Infidel spy, originally a citizen from the outskirts of Ancient Cairo, had been planted in a local market selling food to villagers and Adom's zealous followers. These devoted worshippers, though never officially acknowledged by Panspermia, were known for their fierce loyalty. They often took it upon themselves to evangelize on Adom's behalf after every major rule change or mandate.

The spy strategically befriended leading zealots who had gained temporary access to less restricted areas of Panspermia. Through these connections, he learned of a key detail regarding the blood samples that weren't widely shared. Rumors suggested that more information would be discussed within the Tune, Adom's oceanic stronghold.

According to the intelligence gathered, the blood samples were potentially linked to some form of surveillance. While details were scarce, the implication that the Fortunates desired more than just the ability to cure diseases and extend life was enough to motivate the Vatican to investigate further.

After nearly three weeks undercover, the spy's cover was at risk of being exposed following a dispute with a neighbor. Peter arranged for his extraction back to the Vatican and began formulating a plan to infiltrate the Tune.

Adom had developed a habit of holding his most secretive conversations within an inner court of Panspermia. However, even these walls weren't impenetrable to eavesdropping. The truly secure location was the Tune, situated at coordinates zero-zero in the Atlantic Ocean. It was here that the Endicots and Fortunates residing on Earth managed their rule over the ULE lands. Peter decided this would be his target for infiltration.

While specific details of the infiltration mission were never fully documented in the Scrolls, either due to loss or intentional omission, the story's intensity lived on through oral tradition. It was well known that all others involved in the mission, except Peter, were killed by the Endicots in the Atlantic Ocean.

The plan, as transcribed, was complex and dangerous, requiring patience, careful timing, and extensive surveillance. Peter needed to capture accurate information, as it would be crucial for all future actions. Those involved in the mission are now revered as legends, their sacrifices remembered regardless of potential embellishments to their stories.

Given Peter's recognizable face, he had to find a way to reach Cameroon undetected. His plan involved using prosthetics to disguise his appearance and settle in the area. Labryanthia, unlike Paramatastan, was not as strictly regulated, and uprisings were less common due to the absence of core Infidels. The Fortunates believed the Tune to be impenetrable, which provided some ease once Peter arrived in the region.

The Tune's complex water propulsion system allowed it to hover above the sea, creating a physical and oceanic barrier between it and the nearest land. Despite intense security measures, Peter reportedly managed to get close to the transport barge through a series of distractions both in the water and on the vessel itself.

A fellow Infidel, Andrew, made his way onto the barge as part of the plan. His sacrifice, along with the efforts of those creating distractions in the water, allowed Peter to gain underwater access to the barge. He attached himself to the vessel with the help of the sea team, and although these individuals were later discovered by patrols, the plan to get Peter close enough for entry had succeeded.

The next challenge was to enter through the pressurized water system that kept the Tune suspended and somehow latch onto the structure before being pushed back out. According to the story, Peter grabbed the side of a large vacuum tunnel, allowing the pressure to pull him into a small maelstrom. He navigated through a corridor where water was sifted and funneled, creating a Charybdis-like effect before being expelled.

With only seconds to act, Peter reached out and grasped a small hatch leading to a landing above the waterway. Using all his strength and dexterity, he forced his way through the hatch and rolled onto a metal walkway. From there, he climbed into the Tune's ventilation network, which was barely large enough to accommodate him.

From there, Peter ventured into the Tune's ventilation network. Though designed for someone of a smaller stature, his determination enabled him to squeeze through. Maneuvering through the cramped ducts, he eventually positioned himself above a meeting room filled with familiar voices. Activating a device capable of detecting distant or muffled sounds, he placed it on the vent grate, pressed the record button, and listened intently through the attached headphones.

The conversation Peter overheard was between Ajax, leader of the Endicots. Peter knew this voice intimately, having engaged with Ajax multiple times within the inner sanctums of the Vatican. Those encounters, ostensibly aimed at finding peaceful resolutions to the ongoing rebellion, had always been overshadowed by veiled threats from the supreme Endicot. Regardless, the voice was unmistakable Of course there was Adom's, along with an unknown third party. They discussed the progress of blood sample collection across the various lands, noting resistance in certain areas, particularly around the Vatican. They also revealed that a significant percentage of the samples showed markers of "pure" Martian blood, though Adom expected this number to decrease upon further testing.

The most shocking revelation was Adom's true intention: to identify and extract individuals with pure Martian blood, leaving the "inferior, hybrid creatures" behind. They discussed plans to colonize Mars and potentially exterminate those left on Earth. The conversation also hinted at conflicts on their home planet, Fortuna, from which they were fleeing.

This information was appalling to Peter, confirming his worst suspicions about Adom's motivations. He now had concrete evidence that Adom's purpose was not the progress of Earth, but the harvest of those he deemed "pure" among its citizens.

This pivotal dialogue has been preserved through numerous iterations of the Scrolls, though time has fragmented parts of the message. What follows is the widely accepted account:

Ajax: "We've collected nearly 80 percent of all blood samples. Syricha and Basal have achieved nearly one-hundred percent. A few regions in Labyrinthia remain before we can declare them fully accounted for. Our primary challenges lie in Epocholia and Paramatastan."

Adom: "The Vatican region and surrounding Mediterranean?"

Ajax: "We presume so. The surrounding areas are following suit, and the resistance is growing. After quelling the uprising, we observed a lull in sampling for several weeks. I initiated an aggressive media outreach to the most affected areas, assuring safety and peace. We've seen a slight increase since, but it's not enough to bridge the gap swiftly."

Adom: "Let's persist. Our experts require all samples before drawing definitive conclusions. While it pains me to potentially leave some behind, we must secure a sufficient portion of the population to proceed with construction. Now, what's our status on purity numbers?"

Unknown: "Sir, we have the latest data. The presence of pure, superior Martians among the Earthlings exceeds our expectations. Of the samples collected thus far, nearly 13 percent exhibit pure Martian blood markers."

Adom: "Encouraging news, indeed. However, we must remember that markers alone don't guarantee true purity. I anticipate this percentage will decrease significantly after more rigorous testing. Perhaps this world isn't as degraded and corrupt as we initially believed or as our historical accounts suggested. We're approaching the final phase before departure. I eagerly await the day we rid ourselves of these inferior, hybrid creatures forever. The universe demands cleansing, as it was foretold. Ajax, mobilize your forces to the outstanding lands. It's time we present the Earthlings with a new incentive for providing samples."

Unknown: "May I offer a suggestion?"

Adom: "By all means."

Unknown: "Why not disclose our plans for Mars? We could inform them of our intention to colonize the planet, taking the purest among them. As you mentioned, we only require a certain number for construction. The incentive would be a promise of a better, more prosperous life for them and their families."

Adom: "Wouldn't that incite conflict and confusion? The Earthlings are a proud species. I fail to see how abruptly informing them of their impurity and obsolescence would work to our advantage."

Unknown: "We wouldn't frame it as a matter of purity, but rather one of health. Living on Mars would necessitate close quarters, where any outbreak could devastate the entire population. Unlike Earth, where the infected can be isolated outdoors, the stakes would be higher. This approach could even be perceived as considerate. They needn't know the true motives behind our decision, only that all who provided blood samples are eligible. As they witness their neighbors prospering, their moral reservations will crumble. If not their own, then pressure from close family members may sway those clinging to their beliefs. I believe this strategy will boost our numbers and help us achieve the quota needed to proceed with our other objectives."

Ajax: "And what of those left behind? The ones not selected. Won't they revolt?"

Adom: "Firstly, my dear Ajax, inferior beings require no explanation. We'll placate them with promises of future return, keeping them both compliant and ignorant. This may prove advantageous. Secondly, we'll be long gone should any uprisings occur. When the time is right, they must be eradicated. We'll catch the impure off guard and transport the superior race to Mars. Those who persist in resisting, pure or not, seal their fate. As long as we secure sufficient numbers to aid our construction efforts, we can forge ahead. The universe will soon be cleansed of them. Then, we can finally rest. The entire planet is enthralled by the illusion of peace and prosperity. Why not promise them even greater wonders to come?"

Unknown: "These people are malleable, Ajax. We've dangled enough fortune before them. The remainder can be easily disregarded."

Ajax: "What of the Vatican? If they inquire about our reasons for going to Mars? Won't they demand to know the true purpose? This could fuel further resistance against our sampling efforts."

Adom: "We need not divulge our true motives to anyone. They wouldn't comprehend. We've projected nothing but security and strength here, and I intend to maintain that image. Total purification is essential, even if it means genocide. It will restore balance to the universe, ensuring we never again plummet into darkness, even during unstable times."

Ajax: "And the battles we've lost in our home world? Our Fortunate brethren are perishing on Fortuna's battlefields; it's the very reason for our exodus. What of the purification efforts there? What if our origins are exposed?"

Adom: "That, my friend, would imply a traitor in our midst. And I'm confident these walls are impenetrable to eavesdroppers. Remember, Ajax, we are returning home!"

It was said that while Peter had experienced shock before, this conversation was by far the most horrifying, instilling in him an unprecedented sense of urgency. Though questions outnumbered answers, the recording provided Peter with the ammunition needed to expose Adom's sinister agenda to the masses. It was evident that Adom's objectives were less about Earth's progress and more about harvesting those he deemed "pure" from among its citizens—and the chilling fate he had in store for those deemed inferior.

Exiting the Tune proved as perilous and intricate as entering, but I digress, for these are tales now shared only among the living or passed down through generations.

Suffice it to say, Peter successfully returned to the shores of Cameroon, to the port of Alliance. Once again, lives were lost among the participating Infidels, but their sacrifice has since been honored, their memories enshrined as saints among us.

Upon his return to the Vatican, the paramount concern became how to alert the world to its impending doom. They steeled themselves for the ultimate confrontation with the Fortunates. Before any significant action could be taken, Peter emphasized the necessity of crafting a compelling message backed by irrefutable evidence. This was crucial to persuade the millions of devoted followers across the Lands that their supposed Savior was, in fact, bent on destruction. A vast network of strategically placed informants was deployed, armed with copies of the recording, to disseminate the alarming truth to Earth's inhabitants and unveil this new Age of Deception that had befallen mankind.

As word spread, the world was gripped by fear and confusion regarding their new rulers. With his control tightening its grip on society's fabric, Adom braced himself for what he perceived as the optimal next move.

The world stood on the precipice of division.

"THE AGE OF DECEPTION"

A SENSE OF PURPOSE

The Vatican was emboldened by Peter's recording from the Tune. It was clear to all involved that more nefarious intentions lay at the root of Adom's design for humanity. "Inferior creatures don't need an explanation," Adom had said. The captured statement empowered and fortified all of the so-called Infidels' conspiracy theories, now permanently ensconced in Peter's recording device and in the minds of all who held true to their beliefs.

Truth often came with extensive consequences. The Vatican knew that for this truth to make a difference, it had to be delivered in a way that was believable. It would undoubtedly cause greater division across the lands.

Unfortunately, due to many uprisings and failed coups in the past, the Vatican's reputation among the general public was skewed. Most, having appreciated the Fortunates' contributions to society, considered Peter and his followers radicals Infidels, as they were called in public forums. For the majority of the lands, the Infidels' messaging was simply more propaganda, an attempt to undo the good that Adom had brought to the world.

But now, in their possession, was an affirmation of a reality for which Earth was unprepared. One that made it clear that those dwelling in Panspermia saw no value in most earthlings. Instead, they only wanted to identify the Martian descendants and do away with the lesser creatures. Peter knew from now ancient history books that this thought process was the theoretical foundation that led to potential genocide. When a group of beings looks to purge the world of inferiority, millions must die.

Another piece needed to unfold. The mystery of the Martian descendants. That was the segment of history they were not revealing. What had happened ages ago? That question ran rampant throughout the Vatican regarding that moment of history the Fortunates had not revealed. In Peter's mind, and in the minds of most who were part of the rebellion, they knew this deep down. There was a reason they were drawn to rebel. It was deep seated, but it was there all along. They knew the history in their subconscious. Memories are passed through DNA, and while they span thousands of years, they remain present, shaping who you are. This region especially held those memories embedded within it. The careful placement of Panspermia. Was this where it all began? Was this what some had been stating a while back, that all of this had happened before? Maybe it wasn't just a generic message about empires of the past. Maybe they had seen it within their minds.

It was here where Peter's scriptures began to reveal the power of the memory cells theory. It was passed on to Jacob through writings kept in the vault and eventually transcribed into the scrolls. This teaching continues to be practiced today in hopes that history won't pass us by again. His writings reinforce this throughout, though writings can be lost, destroyed, or misinterpreted. The mind is the true memory bank, and this is what the Fortunates held over the people of Earth. Their teachings were accurate, but as they had done so many times before, they would only release partial truths. While the universe remains the epicenter of all happenings, it is the memory cells that carry its messages.

Memory cells serve as a safeguard, ensuring that not only faith guides us or leads us astray, for the power of remembrance shows us that the universe need not trap us in an endless loop of recurring events. Peter was determined to prevent history from being passed down by others ever again. That remains our daily mission.

This became not just the Vatican's decision but their purpose. They moved forward with great impetus, strategically parceling out the information from them through underground cells of hidden followers. Though not an organized or recognized government, they operated as a cabal. This allowed them to reach people before the Fortunates became aware, spreading their message prior to any media entanglement from the ULE's influenced channels.

Their reach expanded over many years, building a network of silent minorities who recognized truth in their teachings but kept their allegiance secret. Messages passed between them in encrypted cipher, appearing as meaningless text if intercepted. These cells would gather in abandoned buildings or empty parking garages deep within metropolitan areas. Though their numbers weren't great, their influence was substantial due to their clandestine nature. Followers would return to normal activities in broad daylight, subtly sharing ideas with the wider public. The trust they built with fellow earthlings carried the Vatican's message further than any direct approach. When not speaking directly, they planted seeds of doubt, leading others to question everything.

Peter directed the most dedicated cells to share Adom's recorded meeting, highlighting key points when presenting their concerns. These chosen messages spread easily throughout cities. Soon, discussion of this strange recording reached public consciousness. News outlets across all lands broadcast excerpts, though more loyal regions censored much of it. A few regions, primarily those nearest the Vatican in the ancient Mediterranean, allowed the full, unedited version to be heard.

Months after the recording's circulation, this area became a stronghold for the Infidels, earning the name Acre from the public. What began as just the Vatican's immediate vicinity grew along with their influence. The Fortunates' once confident demeanor showed signs of

unease, compelling them to take action. Though initially sporadic, with small pockets of support throughout the Mediterranean region, Acre evolved into a recognized territory. Some considered it a sovereign state, though it continued to follow ULE mandates but only when approved by Vatican authorities. While technically part of Paramatastan without defined borders, Acre developed its own identity. Though the Vatican had Christian roots, Acre's population wasn't primarily religious. They accepted universal teachings but insisted on preserving history regardless of its religious origins.

The uniformed teaching of the universe and its workings was widely accepted, yet history demanded preservation regardless of its religious foundations. The Fortunates would later regret not having abolished it sooner, but that was not to be. And so, Acre flourished in its own way.

Strategically, Adom directed his leaders to reveal more information to quell the growing unrest. Trust needed reinforcement, so they first disclosed the revelation of the Fortunates' former residence on Mars. They revealed that thousands of years ago, they had thrived there. Given their advanced lineage, they described it as paradise to the humans. However, facing impending danger, the Fortunates had chosen to depart their planet, wandering the universe until finding temporary refuge on what would become Fortuna. Their ultimate goal remained returning to their home world.

Adom explained they needed to wait for the universe's timing—a cosmic signal indicating the dangers had passed—and reach an appropriate position in the galaxy that would give the expedition the best chance of locating the Copernican solar system, named after what Earth's inhabitants simply called the Sun. They needed sufficient volunteers to join the search, and those before them would form this group. Yet once again, the complete truth remained concealed.

The span between universal alignments was said to be twenty six thousand years, occurring several times since the original Martian exodus. Those in Panspermia pointed to an ancient civilization's interpretation—the Mayan Calendar— as evidence. Adom revisited the revelation he had shared with the Earthlings upon his arrival. This forgotten celestial map depicted time

circularly, contrary to Earth's adopted linear perspective. He emphasized that humans had once known this truth. Why had they strayed from this understanding?

Adom's teachings astounded humanity. It became evident that throughout ages of worn history, the concept of eras and time itself had been simplified from its purest form to a basic understanding of beginnings and endings. Though he had taught this forcefully before, he insisted people must constantly remember the goal that would benefit all, ensuring the words of the infidels would not prevail. These detractors, he claimed, were sent by the universe in the Age of Iron to obstruct progress.

With this preaching, he hoped to stabilize the lands again, offering a deeper clarification of time as less linear and more cyclical. Adom explained that like a steady pendulum, the universe operated on continuous patterns and expectations. This enhanced Earth's population's understanding, helping them see existence as continuous evolution. Though darkness might fall, light would always follow. While individual destinies remained unwritten, a greater age of enlightenment guided them all.

The universal alignment brought deeper understanding and brilliance. Philosophy flowed more easily, and inherent knowledge seemed more accessible. Adom expressed this to regain Earth's faith, emphasizing again and again that the Infidels were merely universal obstructions being persuaded by the forces during the Iron Age. This was the Fortunates' purpose—to prevent the stars from manipulating minds during this dark period.

Though this information frightened some, making them question even their neighbors' thoughts, Adom promised progression would follow as the stars aligned toward the Golden Age. The Fortunates planted the idea that each twenty-six-thousand-year cycle brought significant change—a new era, worldwide revelation, or destruction.

However, the Vatican recognized Adom's growing sense of urgency as panic. His redundant emphasis exposed the deception taking place. While the alignment occurred as he preached, his claim that the Fortunates alone could guide humanity proved false—a ploy to ensure people heard only one voice.

Yet loyalists still fell at the Fortunates' feet, amazed by their ancient wisdom. Adom declared Earth had reached its lowest point, but progression toward the Golden Age required patience. He continued to emphasize the Fortunates knew how to expedite this process, but first, people must remember their history and recognize their true enemies.

When resistance grew, Adom escalated: everyone must provide blood samples for humanity's protection. Through religious allegories for traditionalists and scientific reasoning for freethinkers, they achieved near-universal compliance. Almost 95% of the population was sampled, allowing the Fortunates to identify those with the purest Martian blood—the chosen few who would return to Mars, leaving Earth to its fate.

As questions mounted and Peter's message spread, the term "Infidels" began to fade. The common people increasingly challenged Adom's words. Though he attempted to denounce the Vatican's claims, Peter's simple question of "Why?" gained momentum. Such a small word, yet it held the power to spark a revolution when asked at the right time. And so, it did.

PARAMATASTAN AND ACRE

Peter had developed an obsessive habit of replaying the Tune recording while deep in contemplation. Others would take this as their cue to exit his chambers, giving him space to process his thoughts. At this time, he grappled with understanding the meaning of a "purer race" and how Martians could be inhabiting Earth. The concept that purity required the destruction of inferiority troubled him deeply.

Then there was the question of utility. Adom had declared that those deemed inferior served no purpose in the Fortunates' plans. But what were these plans, and what role did Earthlings truly play in achieving their definition of *success*?

The voices of Adom and his admiral, Ajax, were instantly recognizable to Peter. Personal messages from the Endicots frequently reached his confines, making Ajax's voice particularly familiar. Video fragments showing Ajax's scowling visage, surrounded by towering alien soldiers, regularly reminded Peter that the

Infidels were violating the treaty and faced imminent extermination. The Vatican had grown weary of that voice.

But the third speaker remained a mystery. This hidden figure clearly held Adom's ear and considerable influence. Had this person been deliberately concealed from Earth? Did even darker plots lurk beneath Adom's facade of goodwill?

These questions wore heavily on Peter's health. Though mentally and physically robust, the burden of truth and its preservation weighed heavily, especially with this newfound evil. The Vatican tried to help Peter maintain his composure, but he had long kept his deepest fears secret. The plan, he realized, had been in motion well before the Summoning.

As blood sample collection neared completion—or at least reached the necessary numbers—the extraction of those with significant Martian ancestry began in earnest. Those with the strongest purity received priority, eager to experience their new world, while those with inferior markers received empty promises and calls for patience. The six land leaders grew increasingly influential throughout the ULE, with Adom maintaining his grip on popular opinion. The leaders preserved their political power through unwavering loyalty to the Fortunates' cause.

Magnus Carter, the appointed leader of Paramatastan, emerged as the most prominent voice. His gift for powerful persuasion elevated him to direct influence under Adom, earning him the *nickname the mouthpiece of Adom* among global media and political circles.

Yet as Magnus's influence expanded, so did the Vatican's opposition throughout his territory. Acre, the sprawling region housing the Vatican, had nearly doubled in size since the leak of Adom's clandestine meeting. The region had generally complied with mandates while consistently exposing the Fortunates' inconsistencies. Though most Earthlings still remained fiercely loyal, Peter's influence and resistance had turned many against the Fortunates. The 13th Legion's efforts to suppress the growing rebellion were failing. The

Vatican's numbers swelled, dividing Paramatastan, and Acre gained worldwide recognition, except from the ULE. Acre had grown so vast that it now encompassed Panspermia itself.

After the first groups of Martian descendants successfully settled on Mars, the six land leaders found themselves regularly traveling between planets to maintain governance. Policing on Mars proved minimal as settlers quickly adapted to their new lives, aided by the Fortunates' superior technology.

To restore order, Adom granted Magnus Carter authority over Earth's law and order. As an Earth native and popular figure, Magnus wielded vast jurisdiction and extreme control, armed with access to Fortunate technology and architects. His public appeals for calm and patience reached every home and gathering space. It took Peter only months to recognize Magnus's voice as the third conspirator from the Tune recording.

This revelation spread rapidly, and those questioning Adom's agenda often found themselves betrayed by their own people. Magnus's support of outside influence over earthly concerns sparked even greater resistance from the Infidels. The Vatican intensified its opposition, growing increasingly militant as Panspermia's influence waned. The resistance spread along the northern coast toward the Mediterranean, though the water created a natural boundary. Panspermia remained an enclave within Acre, though with diminished authority.

As division in Paramatastan deepened, Magnus was chosen to permanently relocate to Mars. He transferred the 13th Legion to govern the peaceful Mars settlers and appointed a new general, Luther, on Earth. Though Luther had led forces during the Vatican incident that claimed nearly fifty lives, his appointment wasn't officially announced until now. With growing rebellion on Earth, a greater show of force was planned. Unknown to the Mars settlers, they had helped construct a new robotic army that would become known as the Battalion.

Battalion Soldiers

Constructed for intimidation and battlefield efficiency, the Battalion Soldiers fulfilled nearly every purpose of their creation. The Fortunate engineers developed two distinct models in their factory-like facilities, using technology exclusive to Adom's kind. Under Magnus's direction, these automated soldiers were equipped with weapons and ballistic gear far beyond human capability.

The standard soldiers, with their sleek black metal design and efficient weaponized arms, became the primary force. Though less intimidating than their counterparts, their simpler design allowed for rapid production and deployment. These troops proved especially valuable as ground patrol forces diminished and Arrow Fighter operations took priority.

The more formidable Berserkers, distinguished by their six weaponized limbs and superior firepower, were originally planned as an elite force. However, their complex design and longer production time led to limited numbers. The few completed units were eventually limited to being stationed within the dome of Tropaion for high-end security. These intimidating machines carried highly explosive projectiles and automatic weaponry powered by advanced Fortunate technology unavailable on Earth.

The Battalion's aerial support came from the Arrow Fighters— aptly named for their triangular, arrowhead design. These remarkable vessels could separate into three individually operated fighters when manned by a full crew. Their silent movement through air and space initially caught Earth's forces off guard, as they had only witnessed them operating as single units. The fighters' pilot pods were designed with versatility in mind, accommodating both Fortunate pilots for transport and Endicots for combat operations.

Luther, a former Earthling who had risen through Magnus's ranks to become his right hand, oversaw the Battalion's deployment to Earth. Like his superior, Luther demonstrated unwavering loyalty to Adom's vision of the future. However, he questioned the necessity of such heavy artillery against his former people. When he voiced these concerns, Magnus's response was swift and stern: fall in line and execute the vision as commanded. As always, Luther complied.

The Battalion operated in two distinct layers. The standard soldiers served as first responders to the rebellion, typically being the only deployed section. Behind them stood the more aggressive, heavily armed Berserker units under Luther's direct command. This second wave wasn't designed to merely subdue uprisings—it represented pure intimidation and aggressive policing, carrying all the hallmarks of an impending war against Earth's population.

The Battalion proved absolutely loyal and trustworthy—not through choice, but through programming. Their deployment marked a significant escalation in the Fortunates' approach to controlling Earth's population, particularly as the 13th Legion transferred to Mars. What had been presented to Luther as a show of force for defensive purposes increasingly resembled preparation for systematic oppression.

MAGNUS AND LUTHER

The story of Magnus and Luther Carter was both purposeful and complex, mirroring their relationship itself. There were so many unknowns about the two that, had people known them more thoroughly, the significant and public affairs that later took place might not have come as such a shock.

While both were known by the masses, Magnus more so at the beginning of his tenure. Their lives contained much undisclosed information. One of those hidden moments happened many years prior to the arrival of the Fortunates and the appearance of Adom. When Panspermia was less known and had only settled in the outer parts of the solar system, closer to the Iron Ages' moment of complete descent, December 21, 2012, of the old Julian calendar—an abduction had taken place.

The abductions were never revealed but were investigated. Though much ambiguity surrounds them, what we now know is that numerous individuals already in positions of power experienced what they would call dreams, but in actuality, they all occurred.

The Fortunates were conducting a series of tests on subjects they could place into positions of power with minimal intervention and effort. These tests would be the inclusion of the same ones they would eventually conduct on all earthlings to determine which had the purest Martian blood. But a greater, more in-depth look into one's own mind was also performed. Thus, through careful identification, Magnus Carter would be the one chosen. So, when the supposed elections began, Magnus was assisted by the Fortunates through media manipulation that made it appear as though the people had truly chosen him, when in fact they were being guided to pick him.

He would eventually hold the position of Senior Representative of Paramatastan and become the ultimate enforcer of that important piece of land that included the birthplace of civilization and the site where the original Martian settlers had begun intelligent life on Earth.

He would eventually sit with the Fortunates and was the first to be informed of Earth's history and how it came to be. Magnus's character had always harbored a sense of superiority, and he readily accepted his role, feeling it was his calling even before it was presented to him. Luther would be a different story, though.

Luther had always been part of the military and showed little interest in politics. His soul was built on morality, and though he was given many chances to prove his loyalty to his Martian blood, he was never told of his ancestry. The Fortunates were constantly perplexed by his actions, expecting his mind would eventually lean toward his inherent superiority, but they remained patient. Having two brothers leading the transplanted earthlings, one as leader and one as military commander, would help the new race of Martians accept all forthcoming plans. This was never to be, for Luther's soul and the universe alike had very different plans for him. The story of Magnus and Luther Carter was a story of its own but should be told by someone who knew the two since birth. The dynamic of their relationship may better explain how two brothers with common hereditary traits developed such different perspectives on life.

Those close to Luther explain that he still privately questioned the presence of such aggressors, given Magnus's plan to maintain peace at all costs. However, the line of communication from Mars to the Battalion seemed to bypass his authority. His word alone was not sufficient, and if the Battalion decided that more aggressive action was needed, they were programmed to deploy the mercenary soldiers. This, too, concerned him as he feared leading an army without supreme control. But his trust in the process and his honor and respect for his older brother kept him from being more aggressive. Still, continued concern weighed on his mind, and he would one day make his voice heard—or this general would step down.

MAGNUS'S AGGRESSION AND LUTHER'S HUMANITY

Even though Luther was placed in charge of the Battalion, Magnus seemed to make the final decisions. Whenever Luther advocated for less aggressive action toward his homeland, Magnus insisted that force was needed. Luther heard rumors of Magnus being involved in the controversial conversations that had spread throughout, but he insisted that his brother would never be part of such acts.

As more prime Earthlings were extracted from their home planet, Mars's population continued to grow, and the permanent colony strengthened. It was now known as Ecopolis—a series of Eco Pods joined together on Mars's surface, similar to Hive City but greater in vastness as the population had grown to challenge the numbers that resided in urban centers back on Earth. It simulated a fully structured urban civilization where the Martians (the transplanted earthlings) and Fortunate engineers worked in unison. A society was formed, and Magnus was now in charge. Though he never voiced his opinion to Adom, he was in fact displeased with being relegated to Mars when he felt his presence was needed back on Earth. Luther became very aware of his irritability and suspected this was behind his overpowering of Luther in many aggressive decisions. Where Luther looked to simply contain a situation, Magnus quickly encouraged more aggressive action. This was constant, and Luther again began to feel the need to challenge. Thoughts constantly entered his mind that maybe there was truth to the circulating recordings, but he couldn't understand why Magnus would have such disdain for his own home. It was also noticed that Adom and his brother had begun referring to Earth as Terra instead.

Magnus recognized Luther's uneasiness with the situation and said there were plans to have Luther work more closely with Terra, as if to appease him.

What transpired next was significant in Luther's continuing apprehension. Many projects were being initiated, and Luther seemed to receive only fragments of information about each. One was even kept entirely from Luther's view. Aside from the eventual unveiling of what would become the Guardians, a major project was being built somewhere between Mars and Earth. It would come to be known as David and Goliath! The pieces were constructed on both Mars and Earth but then transported to a section closer to Mars, though both the completed design and purpose were kept from even those building them.

Adom's engineers worked hard to complete the massive construction of what would be a portal connecting two solar systems across the universe, drawing a large bridge between them. A far more advanced world built by the inherited Martians known as Fortuna would be coming home!

The portal, named David and Goliath, would provide strategic advantage and eventual control for the Fortunates on a much larger scale. As with most developing empires, the desire to expand and reach farther than their own land was intoxicating, but it was more than that. They felt entitled to this land. It mattered not why, but David and Goliath was the tool to do just that. However, this was unknown to the Earthlings and new residents that had currently occupied Mars. The people of Mars had just seen that work was to be done, and as with most, so long as they were providing for their family, they were content. The population is said to have grown to just under a million.

The Guardians

The four Guardians were such massive scientific wonders that it was tragic they were created for destructive purposes—though this was the fate of many innovations. The creators of war machines were often so innovative and visionary that they seemed blind to how their creations would lead to the demise of countless lives. The Guardians were no exception.

Their name was ironic from the start. While they were called Guardians, their posturing and positioning suggested something far different to anyone but the Fortunates—a fact not lost on Luther. The four behemoths were positioned not only between Earth and Mars but in such a way that impurity could not escape Terra and spread its *ungodly* blood and thoughts beyond the world that it currently occupied. The superior Fortunates (ancient Martians) believed that if they could at least have containment and eventual extinction of those that populated Terra they themselves could cleanse the universe. By extracting impurity, it would secure their future so as not to witness and fall victim to their own demise. The universe is one and their survival was dependent on all that existed within it. A theory that was held by their elders. But who decides what is impure and when was that theory born?

Nothing in the Fortunates' plans happened by accident, including the Guardians' coloring. They sat in Earth's outer atmosphere, projecting the four dominant colors of the spectrum: the red of Hades, the golden tinge of Apollo, the intimidating green of Ares that seemed more military than protector, and the brilliant blue of Zeus. Zeus's frame was particularly striking, with noticeable lighting throughout, as it served more as a habitat and operational space station for most of its existence. Once inside any of these massive creations, one would hardly realize the exterior was that of a combative mecha. All excursions between Mars and Earth passed through these great structures. Yet it was the skeleton running through each Guardian that should have caused more fear and alarm than their exterior arsenal—had it been known. And none were more equipped for ending a world and its mortal inhabitants than Zeus.

In the midst of them all sat the absence of light. What the people of Old Earth called the blue marble, the Fortunates saw only darkness—even before the Day of Decimation.

Luther had successfully pushed back against the Vatican on Earth, creating more room for peace and control throughout the six lands. In doing so, he had also given Adom and the Fortunates time to proceed without many setbacks. Though Peter's influence grew stronger, the Battalion's swift counterattacks on the Infidels' terrorist plots made rebellion increasingly difficult. Luther was celebrated among the ranks on Mars, receiving accolades from Magnus and even public praise from Adom on both planets. Thankfully, there had been no need for violent suppression, so Luther faced no mutiny within his ranks. All seemed well, and his position was secure.

That is, until one of his routine meetings with Magnus. After Luther's arrival, Magnus unveiled a plan. It would satisfy Luther's desire for more direct interaction with the Battalion and closer proximity to Earth. The only drawback was that Luther would need to take up a new residence and would no longer live on Mars alongside his brother. He questioned whether this was his brother's doing or came from higher up, beginning to doubt both his brother's motives and his own judgment of events. Reports indicate he continued to follow orders, torn between his moral fiber and allegiance to his brother.

Magnus explained both the purpose of the Guardians and Luther's role aboard them. They were to be free floating machines meant to house combatants' mid space between Mars and Earth, allowing quicker response time to any Earth uprisings. This was Magnus's promise—Luther would be closer to Earth and more hands on in Battalion decisions. The construction blueprints showed them matching Earth's tallest skyscrapers in size. They would serve as both space station and armed artillery, housing Battalion forces with Arrow Fighters and transports to accommodate activity. Collectively known as the Guardians, they were named after ancient gods from humanity's history: Apollo, Ares, Zeus, and Hades. These massive structures would be situated just outside Earth's atmosphere, serving as a security gate managing the predicted increase in traffic between the planets. This was how it was presented to Luther, and while questionable, it seemed logical. They currently moved between planets via Regen pods, but this was deemed too dangerous, with aircraft planned to eventually replace this travel. The machines' only drawback was their slow, lumbering movement—requiring four Fortunates to coordinate their limbs. "So, you see Luther, these are not meant to be warriors, more a home for the Battalion soldiers."

The plan appeared innocent at first, save for one troubling detail. The Guardians were clearly weaponized— even nuclear—created with high-level surveillance capabilities, and most disturbing of all, positioned facing Earth with sights trained on the surface. It was an aggressive posture that Luther found unsettling. A true guardian would face outward from the protected, watching for approaching dangers, or at least rotate to survey the surrounding area. But no—their menacing gaze remained fixed on Earth.

According to Luther, many more aggressive moves seemed planned, but when questioned, Magnus would only say, *All in due time, Luther*. He was told to trust the process. We are told that Luther remained unaware of the ultimate goal of genocide and complete destruction of Earth's beings. We must take him at his word, and his later actions suggested either ignorance or an awakening, though his suspicions grew that more heinous acts were in development. But intuition alone wasn't enough to act upon. Meanwhile, the Hexcorebots were being created and the Day of Decimation approached. Many steps remained hidden from Earth's people, but some believed the Infidels' incidents were accelerating the process. Something was coming, and even high-ranking officials like Luther were kept in the dark.

Those on Earth waited anxiously for their chance at an advanced life on Mars. Most remained unaware they would never join this new breed of humanity. Adom had acquired the necessary workforce for construction, and suddenly halted Earth immigration. They claimed Mars was congested and would soon build new cities to manage population numbers, but in truth, Earth's people were no longer needed. For some time, humanity had celebrated each new construction, announcement, and ongoing development of Mars. Eventually, however, the excitement faded. People began drawing conclusions. Soon they deduced that no more invitations to Mars would come. Migration was effectively suspended, and that's when people pushed back. Peter's words about the great meeting rang louder than ever, and those who remained were not just Infidels—they were Earthlings, and this was their home.

When word spread that David and Goliath would be fully functional within weeks, the "Battle of Gibraltar" would ensure the final exodus would come, whether the Fortunates desired it or not.

CONSTRUCTION OF DAVID AND GOLIATH

The collaborative effort of Mars's new residents was astounding in its organization and seamlessness. The pride they took in completing every task was even more remarkable. They worked the assembly line to perfection, having truly embraced life on Mars and proudly calling themselves Martians. Unfortunately, they remained unaware that every piece of machinery and technological marvel they completed was another step toward genocide, and the construction of Project David and Goliath (PDG) was no different.

Everyone involved felt a sense of accomplishment, yet piece by piece they unknowingly built something that would end lives—lives they knew, people they loved. But this meant nothing to the Fortunates; this was a plan thousands of years in the making. This was their land, and they intended to reclaim it. More precisely, they aimed to rid the universe of unwanted beings who, in their minds, prevented the universe from achieving a constant state of euphoria—a belief passed down through eons.

The pieces were constructed on Mars and, in some cases, in small operations on Earth. Engineers then transported these components to a location between Earth and Mars, closer to Mars's solar orbit, where they assembled them. Goliath, the larger of the two rings, was constructed first, and its completion was cause for celebration. The massive ring measured about a quarter of Earth's moon once complete, and through this gate, David would eventually pass.

While construction proceeded seamlessly, it remained a massive project demanding considerable time and attention. Yet there was a clear sense of urgency to complete it. Peter and his followers noticed this urgency and increased their own accordingly. Something was coming; everyone could feel it. Total completion took another year, but projects moved forward, and next would be the completion of the previously noted Guardians.

BEHOLD THE GUARDIANS

The behemoths known as the Guardians were complete, setting another step toward Earth's final days in motion. Apollo, Ares, Zeus, and Hades were deployed upon completion and sent toward Earth's outer atmosphere.

They hardly appeared to be Earth's protectors. A nervousness now engulfed Earth's remaining people as it seemed this was no longer aimed solely at the Infidels. Earth had become the prison, and its inhabitants the inmates.

Adom still resided on Earth, continuing his attempts to subdue any concerns. Whether people were blind to it all or simply in denial made little difference. While resistance grew steadily, many still chose to believe there were no ulterior motives—that all this was merely to complete their ascension. One must remember that many of Old Earth's people had either passed on or simply forgotten what life was like before Adom and the Fortunates' arrival.

When Apollo landed on Earth, none knew whether this was act of intimidation or a demonstration of mind and technology's power. Apollo, in all its golden might, positioned itself beside Panspermia. Though enormous in stature, people said it seemed less threatening as they gazed upon it. Instead, it became something to marvel at, and then Adom began to speak.

He said something to the effect of: *See, good people of Earth. We bring you protection. We think only of your safety from those who would harm your ascension. These four Guardians are here to keep a watchful eye on all that transpires. With just one of these mighty Guardians, we could have brought down the Vatican, but that is not their purpose.*

The undecided people heard Adom's words and began to sway toward the Fortunates once again. It was true— had they wanted to devastate their adversaries, they could have easily done so, but they hadn't.

Like every move before and every move to come, Adom had acted with precision. He brought the least intimidating of the four to Earth: Apollo, with armor that shone in the sun's reflection and a fierce yet stern face that resembled a golden knight. This was the one chosen, the one people believed to be their protector. But while Adom wasn't entirely dishonest, he revealed only partial truths.

The other three would have appeared more forceful and warlike. Hades was red with a menacing look upon its shoulders, almost as though you'd seen the devil himself. Ares was green and resembled a pure military machine, and then there was Zeus—the largest of all, with an intimidating engineered face atop massive shoulders, coated in thick cobalt blue exterior. Even less known was that Zeus contained weaponry beyond Earth's knowledge and the devastating power it could unleash. Quantum physics lay within Zeus's construction, later revealed as another reason for their journey to their home world's solar system. But no, Apollo was chosen to show the people the Fortunates' supposed genuineness—a guardian in every sense of the word.

The four would hover in space, just outside Earth's atmosphere, but Earth wasn't what they protected. David and Goliath were only weeks from completion and unveiling. As the apotheosis of this crucial portal neared completion, so too did the bridge to mankind's undoing. The bridge to the extramundane world beyond the Copernicus solar system would attempt exactly that.

THE BATTLE OF GIBRALTAR

When the final week of construction arrived for David and Goliath, marking the passage of David through Goliath creating a bridge from our solar system to one of mystery and concern, Mars and its inhabitants planned a grand celebration to mark this historic moment. Even on Earth, in the surrounding area of Panspermia, Adom's stronghold of supporters had planned their own celebration. Many still believed in a harmonious future between worlds. Even those not chosen to go to Mars found hope in this elevation of knowledge and success, dismissing the words of the Infidels as merely that—words.

It was during this time of distraction that the rebels of Earth seized their moment. On the day the celebrations were to begin, they launched their fiercest attack on the Fortunates, initiating a week-long battle through the waters separating the former continents of Europe and Africa. The Scrolls recorded how armies had moved along the coast, gathering numbers in the days leading up to the coordinated attack. They tracked the movement through the lands once known as Italy, Spain, and Portugal. The movement was so well orchestrated that the Fortunates failed to recognize it. This area, while watched, was no longer strictly regulated by ULE rule, as it fell under Acre ruled territory, making maneuvering far easier than in other regions.

The Strait of Gibraltar represented a known weakness to the Fortunates. The northern tip of Africa and southern part of Paramatastan were heavily patrolled by Endicots, with regen hubs placed nearby to quickly summon any of the remaining twelve Legions. However, when martyrs executed the guards and destroyed a portion of the hubs in south Paramatastan, it became clear that the Infidels intended to cross the seven miles of water separating the two lands—and cross they did.

Though the battle claimed many lives for the cause, it ultimately saw the rebels establish a foothold on the old continent of Africa. While still within Paramatastan jurisdiction and north of Syricha, this marked the first time Peter knowingly stood on the same soil as Panspermia and the remaining High Fortunates. The moment drew comparisons to Caesar crossing the Rubicon—there was no turning back, both physically and symbolically, from this relentless challenge to Fortunate authority.

While some labeled them as antagonists who initiated the coming wars, such criticism ignored all that had already transpired. The resistance was real and gaining momentum, with people around the globe cheering the rebels' progress. The Infidels and the Vatican saw the battle as a major victory. Despite heavy casualties and the notable absence of Ajax, watching the Endicots retreat and evacuate for the first time provided tremendous inspiration. Peter and his forces, energized by their success, moved swiftly across the land.

Their triumph was amplified by news of the successful siege of the Tune. Though the Scrolls didn't record the exact process, the tales spoke of how they cut off the water propulsion system, causing the Tune to crash into the ocean. Whether the Fortunates had retreated only because they planned to leave after the David and Goliath festivities remains unknown, but Earth was nonetheless emboldened, and a new pride swept through its people.

Simultaneously, the attack on the town of Alliance, nearest to the Tune set in the Atlantic at 0:0, saw the destruction of more regen hubs. The Infidels' advance across the northern lands so concerned the Fortunates that it provided enough distraction for the Alliance plan and Tune attack to proceed largely unnoticed until too late. Had Panspermia's Fortunates known what was happening, they surely would have prepared for such an attack. This made the smaller rebel band's achievement no less significant—they had seized the Tune, the pristine domed city that had long hovered above the Atlantic waters, now lying conquered on the ocean of crashing waves.

While Earth witnessed the two-day festivities via screen amid this chaos, attention remained fixed on the Infidels' advance, and celebration was short-lived. The disruption of the Fortunates' full accolades brought joy to the Vatican. The celestial ribbon cutting of David and Goliath was completed, and celebrations continued on Mars, where people remained unaware of Earth's events. Their anticipation focused solely on whether contact had truly been made.

Adom pressed on with his speech, furthering the division. He assured Earthlings that confirmation would come soon, and the entire solar system would meet their Fortuna neighbors. Yet observers noted a shift in his tone—the celebration seemed less congratulatory and more concerned. The final exodus was coordinated and completed before further disruption to the Fortunates' plans, but the impact remained significant. They now knew Earth would no longer remain quiet. Whoever crossed through would be unhappy, especially knowing a piece of Panspermia would not exit with the great vessel. While the retreat of the Endicots in the "Battle of Gibraltar" might have been accepted, the seizure of the Tune would not be so easily dismissed.

And so, with this sudden turn of events, Panspermia began planning its exodus. The people of Earth were no longer mere opponents—they had become formidable adversaries.

<u>PANSPERMIA EXITS</u>

For years, Panspermia had made its home just north of the Great Pyramid, but those days were coming to an end. Though they had been reluctant settlers from the beginning, it seemed to Adom that they were now conceding even if this had been the plan all along. The timing escalated, and perhaps for the first time, they were not proceeding according to their preferred schedule. An outside force had made the decision for them.

Preparation for the final days began, though it would not be complete. The Tune was lost, now occupied by many opponents, for the Earthlings had laid claim to it. Though no longer as majestic as before, when it hovered over the ocean with pristine clear glass, its new state—with growing film on its outer shell along with algae and ocean particles—served as both a symbol of victory for the Infidels and one of loss for the Fortunates.

They would soon learn that Adom had others to answer to, and those others would not be pleased with him. He had lost control of the situation when he was so close to working it to near perfection. From the day of his arrival, through all subsequent events, the manipulation had been constant. While always appearing friendly, everything had led to this moment—a plan set in place from the inception of contact, and most likely even before his introduction to Earth's beings.

All Endicots were ordered to gather themselves and return to Panspermia, as many were still scattered across multiple areas of the world at the time of celebration. Everything had escalated as Peter and the Infidels feverishly made their way across the land—this time and not for negotiations but seeking blood.

Media outlets covered both groups, and Peter personally recorded their daily progress. Across the globe, we are told, many lands braced for what was to come. A sense of both nervousness and fear built in all territories. Aside from the area of Acre, most people had enjoyed nearly two decades of peaceful life. To many, this sudden change was terribly unsettling, especially for those who had never known life before the Fortunates destabilized the world.

There were no significant uprisings, or at least none that concerned the people. It was as if everyone held their collective breath. This should have been a joyous time that many had eagerly awaited, but instead, their lives seemed thrown into turmoil and confusion.

The Infidels pressed forward. Though some fell behind needing rest, the majority moved forward with all their might. They met no opposition at this point—the Fortunates were more concerned with preparation to leave. While there would be some political goodbyes, there were no ceremonies; their exodus took priority.

Just as the Infidels came within a marathon's distance of Panspermia, the great ship began to shake the ground beneath it was said to be felt for many miles around. Since their settling, Panspermia had never lifted off, and no one really knew what to expect. Those who witnessed it compared it to a mountain literally excavating itself from the land. With a thunderous boom, Panspermia suddenly took to the skies and then vanished from Earth's atmosphere altogether.

The people below stood gazing into the heavens, even after Panspermia was no longer visible. While there was a collective sigh of relief from Earth's people, more questions than answers remained. Though most of the Vatican celebrated, Peter grew increasingly concerned. He felt that with the Fortunates no longer residing on Earth, the planet lay open for attack with no restrictions. He stared up at the Guardians in the sky and wondered what would come next.

THE ARRIVAL OF THE ELITE

While the days ahead remained mysterious to all, many tried to maintain an ignorant bliss and avoid thinking about it. They continued pursuing their ascension in the universe, believing that even if the Fortunates no longer resided on their planet, they remained part of their world and lives—didn't they? They hadn't totally abandoned them. There were still people on Mars who were friends and family. The Fortunates and Adom were still close by, and more were coming. But they hadn't heard from him since the day they left.

Perhaps this was a test, or were Peter's warnings of genocide really coming to fruition and their days numbered? This question now entered people's minds, though no one wanted to speak of it. The Vatican and firm believers in Peter's findings tried to express the need for action, but they were limited in both resources and options.

They lacked access to the Regen pods that had been sporadically planted throughout the miles between Earth and Mars during the construction period—all had been disabled and destroyed. The Fortunates claimed they were no longer needed, that travel between the two planets was simplified with the stationing of the Guardians, and that maintaining the Regen Pads exhausted their resources. But in the end, it was just another way to limit their inferiors' access to the neighbors and maintain their isolation.

Their only options seemed impossible given their time constraints: either learn the Tune's technology or prepare a fleet of passenger shuttles for their own exodus. With over 8 billion people on the planet and only twenty or so shuttles maximizing 100 passengers at best, the impact would be meaningless. Moreover, where would they go? The shuttles lacked weaponry, making any effort futile. With Battalion Arrow Fighters constantly rotating just outside Earth's atmosphere, even a heroic jump towards Mars would mean certain death. All they could do was wait and stand their ground on their home planet.

Panspermia never touched down on Mars itself, instead hovering close by, even closer to Goliath. Adom made no contact with anyone from Earth during this time— not the people, not the leaders. Terra was left to stand alone and wait. Even Mars residents heard nothing. It seemed the plan had never included settling Panspermia on Mars or becoming one with Ecopolis. Though never stated explicitly, Adom and the others appeared reluctant to join a society containing even the slightest traces of Terra blood, leaving Magnus as their only point of contact. Additionally, someone was coming, and Adom intended to be present for their arrival.

During this time, people overheard Magnus questioning why they waited. Why not attack Earth when they were completely unprepared? They lacked the technology to fight Mars's power. A single strike would suffice—unleashing Zeus and bombing a central location, specifically the Vatican, in his mind. It was there on his own land of Paramatastan that the greatest rebellion had collaborated. Had he had his way, he would have used every weapon the Fortunates provided to crush the rebellion years ago, but there was a greater plan than just crushing the rebellion—the complete genocide of a planet, and someone on the other side of Goliath wanted to witness it.

Then the wait ended. The image within Goliath's ring showed a hazy blackness, a distortion in the star-lit skies of outer space. Suddenly, those of Fortuna made their first appearance through Goliath. A majestic vessel began taking shape through the void. Once completely through, a far more elegant but equally mysterious vessel than Panspermia arrived. The fascinating technology before them helped Earth's people understand that Fortuna might be even more advanced than initially thought.

Made of clear glass and round like a dome, but with technology surpassing the Tune's, the vessel was completely encased. Within the glass stood what appeared to be a city.

The vessel's dome surrounded it with room to spare before narrowing behind into a bridge-like tail leading to a smaller sanctuary dome—undoubtedly either a place of worship or the Keep. The internal city appeared far more complete than the Tune, with larger buildings forming a complete metropolis. It drew power from an unidentified source that gave life to its inhabitants and structures, much like the Tune, but this marvel appeared less dependent on external sources.

The buildings and residences were perfectly shaped, most topped with statues that made the entire structures below appear like trophies or medals for accomplishments. Familiar pyramid structures, both sloped and stepped, stood among them. A building wrapped with a serpent stood next to the Golden Tower in the metropolis center, forming the second tallest structure within the illuminated globe. While the Tune had boasted more subtle architecture, this was by no means a modest city. It was boisterous and large, as intimidating as it was elegant. The vessel was known as Oculus Dexter, and the city it housed was Tropaion, the entire capital of Fortuna—or at least its most significant and important portion. It then became very obvious to all that Adom was just the messenger.

Oculus Dexter

The vessel carrying Fortuna's capital to the solar system of Earth and Mars stood as wondrous as it was distinct—a floating city for all to witness. Created deliberately to showcase the Fortunates' pride in their achievements, it shared similarities with the Tune but on a far grander scale. The dome formed a complete sphere, its underbelly fully enclosed, with a significant bridge extending to the vessel's tail. Within the dome, large structures topped with statues resembled trophies granted for great achievements. Throughout the city stood numerous pyramid shaped structures, both smooth-sided like those of ancient Egypt and stepped like those of old South America.

The vessel embodied both productivity and efficiency while showcasing Tropaion's beauty. They named it Oculus Dexter for its appearance of an eye extracted from one's head—perhaps also a symbolic statement that the Fortunates kept watch over the universe. Its inner glow pierced through the darkness of space like a beacon.

Its unique design allowed it to plant itself in any environment, bringing Fortuna's capital city to any world it chose to settle. The structures within glowed with bright steel, centered around the Golden Tower in the metropolis's heart. When fully enclosed, the darker residence below generated a constant atmosphere for the city above. Upon settling on an alien planet's surface, the lower dome would sit alongside Tropaion, serving as the Endicots' residence.

Once settled on Mars, two tubular tunnels would extend toward Ecopolis's outermost hexagons. Anyone venturing from Ecopolis to Tropaion had to pass through the dark, heavily guarded Endicots' Lair. The entrances and exits were perpetually guarded not just by Battalion Soldiers, but by Endicots themselves—sending a clear message that the transplanted Earthlings in Ecopolis were not considered equals to the new Fortuna arrivals. Few frequented this passageway, as Ecopolis provided sufficient living space for its occupants, but the symbolic division remained clear. Only Magnus, Luther, and the 13th Legion occasionally traversed to the Golden Tower of Tropaion, and even they underwent vetting each time.

The tail section functioned as a bridge, though its true purpose remained mysterious. Many believed it would eventually connect to a larger complex, with the keep at the end serving not just as an anchor on Mars but as a socket for this greater structure—one that no living person had yet witnessed. The metal encased sphere, glowing silver, embedded itself into the ground with functionality beyond mere anchoring. This theory arose from the visual of the panels holding the sphere; before opening into two domes, they were crucial for stability. Once settled, the below city generator created a livable atmosphere for the floating dome above, while the panels extended outward to balance the structure on Mars and filter the external atmosphere for both domed cities. Similar panels appeared at the bridge's end, though the contents of the metallic sphere's dome remained hidden, fueling theories about its true purpose—

especially after Adom's reported retreat there during the Martian surface war.

Adom joined Oculus Dexter's occupants, taking his place once more in the Golden Tower's court. Though the Fortunates originally came from Mars, the atmosphere no longer matched its previous state. Despite ongoing regeneration, it remained unable to sustain life, necessitating atmosphere-controlled environments whether in Ecopolis, Endicots' Lair, or the captivating newly settled Tropaion—a society inclusive by selection but segregated by status.

Upon Oculus Dexter's settlement near Mars, with Adom and several others from Panspermia joining them, an army of Endicots lined the stairs descending from the dome's largest tower. Two gracious figures, Icon and Agatha, emerged to introduce themselves to both Mars and Earth. Their royal status within Fortuna was immediately apparent—both inherently beautiful, strong-bodied, and adorned with the trappings of wealth and status. They were joined by Adom and his top brass.

Unlike Adom's welcoming approach, Icon's speech proved straightforward and curt. After adequately introducing himself and his wife, he left all with one unprecedented statement: "We are here for your preservation. There are others coming for you, be thankful we arrived when we did."

Icon's personality contrasted sharply with Adom's diplomatic nature. He showed no interest in appeasing or comforting anyone, focused solely on his mission with unwavering determination. His mention of "others" introduced new questions Adom had never addressed. Heightening curiosity and unease among Earth's people, who found themselves increasingly shadowed by the looming Guardians, Goliath's portal, and the Fortunates' exodus.

After settling on Mars's surface, with its tail anchored deep below and shells opening to create a second dome, Oculus Dexter established its permanent position. While the Tune had relied on ocean mechanics for propulsion, this lower section appeared to serve as living quarters or, more likely, a defense armory, connected to Ecopolis via a tubular tunnel. Unlike the Tune's reported bird life, the only signs of non-Fortunate life were rumored serpents, perhaps inspired by the Obelisk Ophidian—a tower wrapped in a snake like staircase reaching skyward, later revealed as a place of worship.

Icon's subsequent address, directed solely to Mars's inhabitants, echoed Earth's historical dictators. While meant to inspire pride, it created an unsettling division between Mars's people and their Earth-bound relations.

The speech left many questioning their hoped-for reunions with loved ones left behind.

A crucial meeting followed, attended by Icon, Agatha, Magnus Carter, Ajax, and Adom. Though its exact contents remain unknown, the events that followed suggest its nature. This was no discussion of harmonious treaties between worlds—rather, it concerned the extinction of those deemed inferior. Emboldened by Earth's weakened position and their own might, the Fortunates revealed their true intention: not alliance, but decimation. Adom disclosed that their plan had worked nearly perfectly, positioning them to exploit Earth and eliminate the remaining Infidels and their dying world.

Icon & Agata

The divine couple of the Fortunates had reigned supreme for over a hundred years, and thanks to the banished creator's discovery of micro biotics, they were destined to reign for hundreds more. The pristine duo wore their trademark chromed craniums with delight, and while they appeared android-like, they were anything but robotic. It was said they were considered the most beautiful people on Fortuna, maintaining their distinguished bearing throughout their lives.

Though equipped with the chrome head and fully functional micro-biotics, one thing set Agatha apart from all other females on Fortuna and beyond: she still had golden hair flowing from the top of her head. It was never confirmed whether this was decreed or simply arose from others' fear of copying her style. One thing everyone could confirm was that you did not want to be on Agatha's bad side. Icon was more subdued about it, but he too was someone who should most definitely not be questioned. His cranium was merely etched with the pattern of hair, but even that distinguished him from most others.

It was also well known that while Icon was the King and heir to the royal bloodline, decisions were made as a duumvirate—Agatha's word carried equal power and commanded the same respect as Icon's.

They both came from royalty since birth: he from the capital of Tropaion, where his father was the reigning king; she from Medall, what most called the most beautiful city on Fortuna. As legend had it, the universe had planned for them to rule together, and so the stars aligned. Yet the universe works in curious ways to place you in your destiny—in this case, through the assassination of Icon's father.

After settling in, Icon emerged again, but this time he addressed only the people of Mars. This speech proved far more powerful, reminiscent of Earth's historical dictators, according to the Martian citizens. While meant to inspire self-belief among the people of Mars, something in his words created a stark division between them and the people of Earth. Though the colonists were proud of their relocation, they still maintained relationships back on Earth—friends and family they loved, missed, and had hoped to see again. Icon's speech left them feeling differently now. As soon as he finished, he returned to the Golden Tower.

A meeting followed, and while its exact contents remain unknown, we can speculate based on subsequent events. The attendees included Icon, Agatha, Magnus Carter, Ajax, and Adom—though one notable absence was felt. The discussion had nothing to do with harmonious treaties or trade between the two worlds. This was about the extinction of what they deemed an inferior being—about cleansing the universe, something they believed should have been done three cycles ago. Emboldened by Earth's weakened position and the Fortunates' demonstrated might, this arrival wasn't about an alliance with Earth but rather its ultimate decimation. Adom revealed that their plan had worked nearly perfectly, and they would finally exploit Earth for what it was and lay waste to the remaining "infidels" and their dying world.

Luther reportedly struggled internally as he learned fragments about Icon's arrival and its moral implications, given his human heritage. Though not privy to the extreme details, we're told he attempted to negotiate against every severe action demanded of him. One thing became painfully obvious over the following days: the Fortunates cared nothing for Earth's preservation, only their own advancement.

He overheard them speaking with disdain about the people of Terra, as if nursing an ancient vendetta against the entire race. Only his brother's apparent thirst for the same goal kept Luther maintaining his allegiance. He wondered: was his brother seeing something he couldn't, or did he possess withheld information? If so, why?

And there it is again—that simple question that stimulates the mind like no other. The Fortunates' arrival left Luther and many others with more questions than answers. Adom had never mentioned any "others" that Icon referenced in his attack. Was it a lie? Or was Adom protecting them from a truth—that all of this was for their protection? Luther recalled the meeting where he heard that the Vatican had spread, wondering if this connected Ajax's cryptic comments about events unfolding on Fortuna. In such moments, one must search within and remember all that has been heard.

THE VATICAN RETHOUGHT

Reclaiming the land of Paramatastan proved essential in restructuring both the Infidels and Earth itself. An aggressive temperament had swept across the lands. With Magnus now taking full residence on Mars and the Fortunates no longer occupying any Earth territory, one of the core regions had been left without true appointed leadership. Adom's words no longer carried the weight of law within the U.L.E., creating an opportunity for the Vatican to step into power. Before chaos could take root, realignment was necessary. Though perhaps not as rigid as under the Fortunates' rule, the Vatican and Infidels swiftly moved to establish order.

Some of their actions might have seemed aggressive, such as the renaming of major cities—drawing from the Roman Empire, Istanbul once again became Constantinople. People worked tirelessly, constructing walls and castles. During this transition, a man named Zachary Damir began to make his voice heard, sharing his opinions and strategies. He formed an alliance with Peter and soon became the one people turned to for answers. The Vatican became the new capital of Paramatastan, and while never officially appointed, Zachary gradually assumed the role of Pope— or so his nickname suggested. This wasn't a religious coronation; rather, it represented the planet's need for protection and recognized order.

Though one might have expected Peter to lead, it wasn't in his nature. At his core, he was a soldier, meant to lead on the battlefield.

The restructuring of this confused state finally found a clear voice. While the structured government remained intact, its appearance shifted from that of a republic to something more akin to an empire. This transformation wasn't achieved through force but through words and ideology, which the surrounding lands seemed to embrace. The cultivation of national pride can have such effects, especially when the right person repeatedly emphasizes an "us versus them" mentality. Soon, the Vatican came to be regarded as the world capital. Though the names of the original continents were never fully restored, neither were the more recent U.L.E. designations. While division wasn't readily apparent, it was a world of complexity that had somehow unified within itself—all its inhabitants simply known as Earthlings. Traditional borders faded away.

Mars took notice of these movements, and during this period, power struggles reportedly emerged. Magnus called for swift action as he witnessed Earth's new positioning, convinced they were preparing for potential war with Mars. Icon, while equally aggressive, preached patience—born from his confidence that their day of reckoning was approaching, and nothing the people of Terra could do would halt what was already in motion. Adom had retreated into the chain of command, aligning with Icon's position and maintaining silence otherwise.

Luther's strike force proved the most strategically placed to keep Earth's people in check, constantly monitoring and reassessing all terrestrial activities from the guardian known as Apollo. The Battalion made occasional visits for closer observation, but no strikes were executed. Luther recognized his brother as the aggressor, suspecting that power had simply gone to his head, still bitter about failing to contain the Vatican's growing strength in the territory under his command. From the fragments of conversation Luther overheard, it seemed Icon was willing to accept a divided worlds scenario, provided no further aggressive actions took place under his rule. Luther remained unaware of the larger plan, and many believed Magnus was equally in the dark—until the day the Hexcorebots were unveiled.

THE PLAN ALL ALONG

It is estimated that around 41 AD (or June 19, 2053, on the Julian calendar preserved with the scrolls), a meeting was called—this time, even Luther was summoned to Mars.

This event would later be known as *The Day of Decimation* marking the death of a planet, with the Hexcorebots as its executioners. The following account is based on Luther's words.

There was a sense of both exhilaration and accomplishment in the room. Icon and Agatha sat at the head of the gathering in thrones. Also present were his brother Magnus, along with Adom, Ajax, and Echo. A few others attended, but Luther did not yet know them— although there were many Endicots in attendance. Perhaps their unease stemmed from what was about to be revealed; only Luther and Magnus, born on Earth's soil, had once called Terra their home.

Icon proceeded to introduce six large, ominous robots intended for Terra. Their frames were forged from a metal unknown to Earth, called coin-run on the periodic chart. The robots were designed to drill toward the Earth's core, withstanding the immense pressure of each layer—from the mantle to the inner core. Upon reaching the core, the robots would detonate, ensuring the planet's destruction.

The resulting explosion would unleash gases into the atmosphere, poisoning the skies. Those closest to the eruption would perish instantly, while others, regardless of distance, would eventually succumb to the fumes. The toxic air would spread, dooming all life on the planet. This was the devastation orchestrated by the Fortunates, and Icon and Agatha had gathered to witness it firsthand and revel in its execution.

Luther objected to the plan, but his protest fell on deaf ears. This wasn't a debate—it was simply a briefing. He and Magnus were made to understand that, from this point forward, they would have no family beyond the Fortunates and the transplanted Earthlings on Mars, to whom they were related. The Carter family's Martian bloodline ran deep.

It was unclear whether Magnus shared Luther's moral outrage. If he did, he quickly suppressed it, embracing the plan. From that moment, Luther was under constant surveillance, leaving him no choice but to comply. He wasn't told the exact timing or location of the attack. Meanwhile, those on Earth, unaware of their fate, would soon be plunged into panic, with no chance of escape.

All Luther could think of was that Mother Earth was doomed, along with her nearly eight billion children.

Meanwhile, Peter, driven by intuition or foresight, took drastic steps to prepare. He escalated every defensive effort possible, knowing that the Golden Age of Earth, once promised by Adom, would never come. He and his followers fortified the region where Panspermia had once flourished. There was significance in that location, though Peter couldn't fully understand it—only that the Fortunates never acted without purpose.

Hundreds of thousands of people gathered throughout the region, preparing for the inevitable. Though it seemed like a futile effort, they refused to believe that. Over the years, Earth had been stripped of its nuclear weapons by the Fortunates, and treaties with the U.L.E. left humanity with a limited defense—tanks, fighter jets, and warships that paled in comparison to what they would soon face. They had no idea what their enemy created and even if they did it would defy all comprehension.

In a final, desperate act, Luther attempted to contact the Vatican. His message was simple: Evacuate. Whether the warning reached anyone on Earth remains unknown, and even if it did, it's uncertain how it was received. As Earth's field general, Luther's message may have been mistaken for an order rather than the dire warning it was meant to be.

Ultimately, it wouldn't have made any difference.

DAY OF DECIMATION

According to the Scrolls of Jacob, the sky resembled a metallic shadow, held together by the fasteners and welds of alien machinery. Vessels hovered across the Northern Hemisphere in an aggressive formation, poised to unleash devastation upon the surface below.

Every day, new carriers arrived within Goliath's field, ferrying Fortunates from Fortuna to Mars. The Martian population grew rapidly, and with it, the planet's infrastructure expanded to accommodate the influx of settlers.

The plan to decimate Earth was carried out discreetly, without visible reinforcement from Fortuna's allies or rather, contacts on Earth. Adom's once-cordial tone faded from the voices of those left on Earth if they heard from him at all. The Infidel's influence spread unchecked, and the truth became evident through action, not words. As unrest and panic swept the lands, it became clear that those remaining on Earth were viewed as inferior—a lesser race, unworthy of the Martian legacy.

A final council was held on Mars, attended by Adom, Icon, Ajax, Magnus, and Luther. The decision had been made Earth was no longer of any use. Everything important to the Fortunates had been extracted, leaving only ashes and inferior blood behind.

Luther was assigned to lead a battalion of soldiers to one of the four Guardians floating behemoth structures encircling Earth on a barge called Tundra. Upon arrival, the Tundra would dock with the Guardian, and Luther's battalion would disperse to the other Guardians. Unlike previous missions, Magnus would accompany him this time.

After the battalion secured their posts, an armada of Arrow Fighters was deployed—more than Earth had ever seen or imagined. The sky darkened as black and silver aircraft filled the heavens, especially above the Mediterranean region. Then, a lone ship descended into Earth's atmosphere, crashing into Mesopotamia, an ancient region known to Earthlings.

This ship was commanded by Ajax, accompanied by a handful of low ranking Endicots. Inside the transport, the Hexcorebots lay dormant, waiting to carry out the destruction they were built for.

As the transport gates opened, the Hexcorebots emerged, surrounding a team of Endicots who swiftly assembled a smaller version of the regen stations with surgical precision. One by one, the Hexcorebots stepped onto the now active pad and were transported to strategically placed regen hubs in a hexagon formation across the lands once known as Saudi Arabia, Egypt, Turkey, Syria, and Iraq.

Once in position, the Hexcorebots arranged constructed bodies into a diamond like formation and began drilling furiously into the Earth's crust, their goal: the gaseous mantle and core beneath the surface. Small bands of Endicots guarded the drilling sites, while Arrow Fighters patrolled overhead, circling like a murder of ravens.

The Hexcorebots

The Hexcorebots were created with a singular purpose. Unlike other constructs born from the Fortunates' grand designs, these six machines were conceived after they had already settled near the pyramids of Cairo. And as we later learned, this choice of location was no coincidence. When the earthlings welcomed the Fortunates, believing they were extending hospitality to friends, they unknowingly invited the devil into their home.

It became common for the Fortunates to roam the surrounding lands, studying the soil and the air. At the time, few noticed that their exploration was confined to a specific region: the Middle East and the Mediterranean. Their plan was to extinguish civilization precisely where it had first emerged. This land had once been home to the ancient Martians who had arrived thousands of years ago, laying the foundation for Earth's earliest communities. While the Day of Decimation was intended to end civilization, it also revealed long-sought answers to Earth's mysteries.

People had always wondered how primitive tribes evolved into organized societies and why so many ancient structures remained. It was the abandoned Martians who had taught early humans, likely for their own survival. Evidence of their influence remained drawings of spaceships, inexplicable scientific knowledge far ahead of its time. But, as with all histories, the truth became distorted over time, slipping into myth.

The Fortunates were determined to drive a dagger into the heart of the planet. To do so, they deployed the Hexcorebots, which were built using alien minerals unavailable on Earth. The original plan was simple: they intended to drill deep into the Earth as though mining, slowly poisoning the planet from within. But when resistance from the earthlings escalated, a new strategy emerged—one that called for speed and precision.

The Hexcorebots were designed to accelerate the drilling process through a coordinated attack. Rather than bore into one location, they would drill in a hexagonal pattern across vast regions. Each bot's angle of descent ensured that their paths would eventually converge near the Earth's core, triggering a catastrophic explosion that would shatter the crust. This synchronized devastation would usher in the Day of Decimation.

However, just as the humans failed to comprehend the Fortunates' initial objectives, the Fortunates themselves failed to anticipate the chaotic gases hidden deep within the Earth. They considered themselves pure beings— but Earth, in its own way, had always harbored its own vision of purity. And purity, it seemed, depended entirely on one's perspective.

From above, Luther observed with grim clarity. Every reconnaissance mission, every soil sample—it all led to this moment. The Fortunates had carefully orchestrated the planet's downfall, and now the pieces had fallen into place. But there was deeper symbolism at play. The Fortunates chose the very region where the original Martians had landed, where civilization had first blossomed after the Iron Age's collapse. What the Martians had created long ago, they were now destined to destroy.

As Peter had feared, the battle lines were drawn in the same region where humanity's story had begun. In Cairo, the earthlings launched a desperate counterattack, fighting with everything they had. Fighter jets lit up the skies, but they could not outmaneuver the Arrows three pilot ships that could split into separate fighters' mid combat, overwhelming its opponents. On the ground, the battle was equally fierce. Even Apollo, once revered as a symbol of hope, lumbered through the battlefield. Though massive and slow, it functioned as a mobile fortress, unloading battalions of soldiers directly into the heart of Jerusalem.

Meanwhile, the Endicots, stationed aboard barges in Iraq, rushed to defend the drilling sites. Their mission was to protect the integrity of the Hexcorebot's operation and fend off intruders. Toxic gases—burning with nickel and iron—were intended to poison Earth's atmosphere, wiping out all life. It was then revealed that the Hexcorebots carried nuclear detonators. If they reached the planet's volatile layers, their detonation would trigger geysers of death, flooding the surface with molten destruction.

The fight became a brutal, close quarters melee. Endicots, battalion soldiers, and humans clashed in a desperate struggle—each side determined to either save or destroy Terra. As the body count rose, Peter realized that his son Jacob would soon be drawn into the heart of the conflict, fighting beside him to the bitter end.

The Infidels, now hailed as heroes, rallied under Peter's command. The

Vatican's core forces joined the resistance, forming militias to repel the oncoming doom. Though Adom and his leaders had prepared for retaliation, they had not expected the scale or precision of the earthlings' counterattack. A data breach had provided them with vital intelligence—locations, timetables, and weaknesses—and the result was an all-out war. Battles erupted across Cairo, the Gulf of Suez, and beyond. The fiercest fighting took place at a drilling site just south of New Cairo City, where martyrs hurled themselves into the hole, laden with explosives, in an attempt to destroy the Hexcorebot.

Hours into the battle, as the Hexcorebots relentlessly drilled deeper, a moment arrived that would go down in history. Through the chaos, Ajax and Peter found themselves face to face. They had crossed paths before, but those encounters were civil. On this day, no words would be spoken. The battlefield fell silent as both armies paused to witness the confrontation—a duel that would be remembered for generations.

Ajax, a towering figure with unmatched strength, wielded Jupiter, a sword of vitality. Yet Peter fought with the unrelenting heart of a warrior. As Ajax struck Peter repeatedly, it became clear that the end was near for the man known as Peter DeLuca. With his final strength, Peter sought out his son, Jacob. When their eyes met, Peter tore the chain from his neck and placed it in Jacob's hands.

At first, the gesture seemed sentimental—a father's farewell. But the charm on the chain held something far more valuable: the code to access Peter's writings. As Ajax prepared for his final blow, Peter whispered to his son, *Do not let them tell their story. Run.*

Jupiter's blade sliced through Peter, from neck to waist. As Ajax delivered the fatal strike, Peter closed his eyes for the last time. Those who witnessed the moment later claimed that a look of peace crossed his face, as if he knew that Jacob would carry on the fight. And with that, the restless warrior finally found eternal rest, both in life and memory.

The tides of battle began to shift, and the earthlings soon realized that they were fighting a losing war. Endicots and battalion forces pressed forward, driving the resistance further back. The fight became one of survival. Though many wished to keep fighting, the reality of defeat weighed heavier than their cause. Slowly, the retreat began—first in hesitation, then in full flight, as the ground itself seemed to crumble beneath them.

Eruptions tore through the battlefield. Lava spewed from the drilling sites, while toxic gases seeped from the Earth's core. Brave men and women, who had moments earlier believed they stood on the pinnacle of life, now faced the horrifying truth: Adom —the voice they had once welcomed— was the harbinger of death.

The Endicots fled to their vessels, but many were left behind. As the ships ascended, the survivors watched Apollo race alongside them, crammed with as many fleeing soldiers as it could carry. Those left behind choked on the poisonous fumes—their Martian blood betraying them in the end.

From the sky, the devastation became clear. A massive crater stretched across the Middle East, a gaping wound that resembled a gunshot to the heart of the planet. The Day of Decimation had come to pass—but to what end?

Were they witnessing the death of their world? Or the stirrings of its rebirth? In the aftermath of destruction, it seemed that Mother Earth had plans of her own. And, as with all life, survival is merely the beginning.

<u>TERRA REBORN</u>

Can you really kill a planet without reducing it to mere rocks and ash drifting aimlessly through space? Or will life find a way?

The devastation was unimaginable. No more screaming. No more sirens. Only the tears of those who remained. Subtle explosions echoed across the lands, but they were no longer from combat. They were the dying breaths of Terra's core, seeking release wherever it could. Toxic gases spewed from the crater carved by the blasts, blotting out the skies. The inner earth erupted violently, launching debris and molten rock miles beyond the detonation site.

Many perished instantly, scorched by the core's fury, while billions faced a slower, inevitable doom. Their lungs filling with the smog and soot that now blanketed the planet.

Fort Vatican

For centuries, the Vatican had stood as the sacred heart of Christianity. But in the years leading to the Day of Decimation, its significance evolved. It became more than just a religious sanctuary—it was a symbol, a fortress of knowledge and history preserved amidst chaos. Those who sought refuge within its walls did not always believe in the old faith, but they clung fiercely to what it represented: resistance against surrendering to the lies of the new order.

Among the significant figures within Fort Vatican were Peter and his son Jacob, soon joined by others like Zachary and eventually Cornelius. Together, they formed a community of purpose, a calling that went beyond faith, something that even the Pope struggled to define. And when the Pope was assassinated during the raid, the inhabitants knew they had to fight for what was theirs. The Vatican was reborn—an unofficial yet deeply symbolic bastion now known as Fort Vatican.

After the Day of Decimation, the transformation was complete. Gun turrets lined the walls to fend off air raids, including the Battalion's Arrows, while statues of the risen world Apostles adorned the battlements, their stony gazes serving as guardians. But these statues did not merely protect the structure—they guarded the spirit of the Earth itself, a reminder of what the planet meant to those who remained.

Fort Vatican stood as a beacon for those who refused to abandon their home. It was not just a city but a symbol of Earth's enduring spirit, and the survivors would fight with all they had to protect it. For just as Terra had given them life, she would offer one final chance for redemption, and they would answer her call.

The weight of what had transpired settled heavily on Luther as they returned to Mars. Though most of the transplanted earthlings were unaware of the massacre, an unsettling sense lingered—something malevolent had unfolded. As the 13th Legion greeted them with silent nods, Tundra's return only deepened the eerie atmosphere.

Ajax strode through the crowds toward the corridors of Tropaion, his expression cold and unreadable. Magnus, on the other hand, wore a subtle grin, a flicker of satisfaction creeping across his face. The mission was complete. The Fortunates were ready to embrace their heroes.

In the following days, the Guardians remained stationed over Terra, observing the planet's slow demise. But to everyone's surprise, life endured longer than expected. Animals roamed freely, unaffected by the toxic air that was supposed to extinguish all life. Even a few humans, scattered across the land, continued to survive—defying every scientific prediction.

The Fortunates were baffled. If animals could breathe, why not humans? Though starvation claimed many, the air itself was not killing them. Magnus urged the council to authorize a final extermination, but the Fortunates dismissed his pleas. To them, prolonging the suffering was part of the victory.

Back on Mars, the transplanted earthlings grew restless. They demanded answers, and crowds gathered daily outside Magnus's quarters. Magnus, being the most accessible of the leaders, was forced to face them. Yet, behind his growing frustration lay a grim determination—to finish what they had started.

On Terra, a strange new reality was emerging. Though billions had perished, those who survived felt an unexpected surge of vitality. Against all odds, they grew stronger with each breath, as if Terra herself was empowering them to endure.

The remaining survivors began to gather, searching for loved ones, and though many found only graves, their quest brought them to others. An unspoken instinct guided them toward the Vatican. It was as if the Earth was calling them to unite.

Even more astonishing were the changes within the survivors. Some discovered abilities they had never known—lighting flames with a snap of their fingers, moving objects with their minds, even defying gravity through flight. It was as if Terra, in her final moments, had gifted them with the tools to fight back.

With most communication networks destroyed, the survivors relied on newfound mental powers or faint whispers from the Earth itself, guiding them to the cavernous crater left by the explosions. Along the way, many stopped at Fort Vatican, drawn by the presence of Zachary Damir, once the Vatican's voice, now rumored to possess powers of his own.

As the survivors continued to converge, they spread across the Mediterranean and the ancient lands of Mesopotamia, seeking answers and a purpose.

Despite the devastation, some of the planet's oldest structures endured— The Pyramids, the Great Wall of China, and even the newly fortified Wall of Jacob in Constantinople. Though scarred by the explosions, these landmarks stood as a testament to the Earth's resilience. Some whispered that it was not mere architecture but the will of Terra herself that kept them standing.

Earth was reborn, transformed into a land that resembled an ancient, Arcadian world. With technology in ruins and society reduced to its most basic elements, the survivors found themselves living in a world that mirrored old legends. What were once myths of sorcery and strange creatures now seemed all too real.

The Vatican stood at the heart of this transformation—a place of both refuge and power. And though the skies remained dark, and the land mourned its losses, the survivors knew they were far from defeated. The "Scrolls of Jacob" would chronicle this new era, ensuring that the mistakes of the past would not be forgotten.

The darkness of this new age was not one of despair but of transition. And as the survivors adapted to their strange new world, they realized that their time on Earth was far from over.

Reports from Earth reached Mars, and the news shook the Fortunates. Terra's air, which they had believed lethal, was not killing the survivors. Icon, infuriated by the miscalculation, ordered the execution of the chief scientist responsible for the failed prediction. In accordance with the teachings of Adom, the second in command scientist quickly assumed leadership, tasked with understanding this new phenomenon.

With Terra defying expectations, the Fortunates deployed a wave of Battalion forces, accompanied by Luther and a squadron of Endicots. Their mission: to rendezvous with the Guardians and launch an invasion of Earth.

The battle for Terra was far from over. And as the survivors on Earth discovered their newfound powers, they knew that the time had come to defend their home—no matter the cost.

Jacob

The son of Peter DeLuca grew up not knowing any other way but in the shadow of the Fortunates. Yet, from a young age, he found himself opposing them—not just out of loyalty to his father's defiance but from something deeper, something that felt like destiny. It was as though he carried a purpose beyond what was taught—a drive to resist, to preserve what was slipping away. Like many others of his time, Jacob fought not just for survival but to remember why they fought, to preserve a legacy.

Growing up, he observed his father closely, and these thoughts weighed heavily on him. It often seemed as though Jacob knew not only what had happened but also what was about to happen. Perhaps that's why history remembers him sitting upon the throne behind the Wall of Constantinople, his mind endlessly calculating how to alter a fate that seemed inevitable. There, he would contemplate the future, often gripping his sword and spear as if he were always prepared for battle—or perhaps it was merely the image history imprinted on the collective mind.

Like the legendary Ajax, Jacob wielded famous weapons—Lux, his sword, and Nox, his spear. Though the ancient scrolls never explicitly mention it, rumors persist that both were forged from the rare coin-run metal from Fortuna. If true, it remains a mystery how Jacob came to possess this resource. The weapons were said to slice through any material with unmatched ease, and their grips, made of pure stone, aligned perfectly with his power to manipulate the earth. Where others found the weapons unbearably heavy, Jacob wielded them effortlessly, channeling his abilities to increase their speed and impact with each strike.

But Jacob's strength was not enough to fend off the creeping darkness. Even he admitted that the skies grew black and the abyss before him seemed even darker. Yet, he kept his father's promise alive, preserving their story—an essential history that would later guide Zachary. Jacob knew that telling the story was as crucial as fighting. Tell the people, Zachary, he said. Even if this world ceases to exist, the lessons we learn in these dark times must endure, or they will be repeated.

Many have wondered: did Jacob always know how the story would end, even before it began?

The group that returned to Earth after the Day of Decimation was smaller-sent not for conquest but to investigate what remained of the planet. Magnus urged them once again to deploy the Guardians and wipe out the Earthlings, but Icon resisted. Magnus, growing increasingly frustrated, couldn't comprehend why Icon hesitated to sacrifice even a single Guardian. It was as though Icon had another purpose for the Guardians, something far beyond the destruction of Terra.

Meanwhile, Luther arrived at the Zeus station, dispatching a team to Earth alongside several scientists. Their mission: collect samples of air, water, and soil. However, they avoided the Vatican, fearing reports of Earthlings developing supernatural powers. A confrontation with such powers was too risky. The team landed on what was once known as Russia, now part of the fallen Labryanthia during the final days of the ULE.

The plan was to stay there briefly, but what happened next stunned them all. As soon as the vessel's doors opened, the scientists and accompanying Endicots collapsed, gasping for air, and died within moments. Only the Battalion soldiers remained unaffected, their nonorganic forms immune to the strange atmospheric shift. Every Fortunate perished. It was as if Earth itself had rejected their presence.

The one known as the Omniscient 1—though blind—reported on the event, claiming she saw everything clearly in her mind. She spoke of memories from the beginning of time and glimpses of what was yet to come. Luther recalled the Battalion and ordered them to collect the samples as planned. As he gazed out at the planet that had once been his home, he realized Earth was no longer the world he remembered.

The cities that once pierced the sky had crumbled. Smoke filled the air, and the landscape resembled the darkest periods of history, like the Middle Ages—an age of sorcery and fear, now no longer mere legend. Some

Earthlings could summon fire with a gesture or command lightning with a word. Smog, swords, and sorcery replaced technology and peace.

Pope Zachary Damir assembled a group to uncover the source of these newfound powers. Zachary himself wielded control over the elements, and when Jacob burst through the gates of the Vatican, hope was rekindled. Together, they knew that new legends were about to be written.

Jacob's power to move the earth with mere gestures and Cornelius's ability to jump through time formed the foundation of the Core. They set in motion plans to rebuild, meeting in structured councils. As more survivors gathered around the Vatican, their numbers grew to over a million. Yet they could not forget that billions had perished. Zachary and Jacob reminded them that dwelling on losses would only weaken their resolve. Those who survived had a purpose—a reason to live.

To avoid another catastrophic attack, they spread their population throughout the region. Pope Zachary held the Vatican, while Jacob took residence behind the Wall of Constantinople. They searched tirelessly across the planet for survivors, though most claimed to have been drawn to this area by an inexplicable calling. Still, they scoured the Earth to ensure no one was left behind.

The Fortunates, observing from Mars and within the Guardians, began to take notice of the unity forming among the Earthlings. From above, they saw people coming together—not as scattered individuals, but as a single force bound by the identity of Earth.

Jacob took it upon himself to protect the writings of his father. Beneath his throne behind the Wall of Constantinople, he placed an ark containing his father's records, ensuring that Earth's story would be told, not just the version written by the Fortunates. A man known only as Clone—capable of replicating himself up to twenty times—painstakingly transcribed Peter DeLuca's writings, creating hundreds of scrolls. These scrolls were distributed across the land, ensuring that no part of their history would be lost.

Meanwhile, on Mars, scientists struggled to analyze the samples they collected. After repeated failures and mounting deaths, Luther suggested that Earth was rejecting the very blood of the Martians, defending itself from its former invaders. His hypothesis sparked debate but was met with urgency. Had they studied the landscape more closely, they would have realized that only one species— serpents—had failed to survive on Earth, hinting at a far deeper connection to the planet's ancient past.

The people of Earth pursued similar questions. However, their confidence in their newfound abilities occasionally led them astray. Zachary and Jacob constantly reminded them to remain vigilant—their struggle was far from over.

One voice stood out: a warrior known as Warlord. "We *were given these gifts for a reason*, he declared. *I'll be damned if I don't figure out what that reason is—and use it to protect our people*." His words ignited a spark among the Earthlings, awakening them to the realization that they were part of something far greater than themselves.

And so, a plan was forged. Those with extraordinary abilities gathered, forming a new alliance. What had once been the stuff of fiction —heroes drawn from stories for entertainment— was now becoming a reality. The age of superheroes had begun.

APOSTLES COMETH

A gathering began at the Vatican for the most part, but some traveled to the Wall of Constantinople, eager to demonstrate their newfound talents to Jacob. They were not there merely to show off their abilities; they all wanted to be part of the front line defending their homeland—Earth. Anyone could fight if called upon, but a select group would undergo training to become a cohesive team. This is how you defeat an enemy: through strategic collaboration and by complementing a peer's weaknesses with your strengths.

Apostles Hall

On the day the Infidels pushed back their opposition and set foot in Old Earth's Africa after the Battle of Gibraltar, an equally significant moment occurred—they seized the Tune. While some believed that the Battle of Gibraltar was indeed a pivotal moment, others wondered if the Fortunates had pulled back due to an already planned exodus, aiming to retreat with as many of their forces intact and avoid further casualties. But the seizing of the Tune could not have been part of their plans.

The Tune was the center of Panspermia, and though the fuselage remained capable of full functionality, it must have served as a constant reminder whenever a Fortunate walked through its grand halls. When The Day of Decimation arrived, it was not even a concern for the Fortunates, as the eco dome housed minimal life. Yes, they were proud of their moment of victory, but it offered little convenience to those residing in it, as all goods would need to be shipped to the island eco dome.

During the seizure, they had to destroy the functioning mechanics below to gain access, rendering the city that was previously self-reliant unable to sustain itself. It drifted in the Atlantic Ocean, now just a symbol of victory, while its pristine habitat began to deteriorate, collecting seaweed and debris along its edges, with the dome becoming clouded.

However, as the people of Earth rose and embraced their newfound gifts, the Tune was eventually restored to a functioning fortress, now known as Apostles Hall. Though it would never return to its former pristine days, it became the home of some of the most famous individuals on the planet until its final days. Both Apostles I and Apostles II called it home. Beneath Apostles Hall, Tiburon would be housed until its unveiling, and it was where the Apostles would train and strategize.

At the time of its occupancy, it provided the people of Earth with three significant strongholds: Fort Vatican and the Wall of Jacob were its companions. It represented a rising in the new inhabitants and served as a glaring reminder to their alien friends that the place they called Terra had now claimed one of their own pieces of technology as their own.

__Footnote__: Two of the first Apostles streaked through the sky. Ra, a young lady from India, developed the power to channel the sun through her body. It was almost as if she were one with Copernicus, as her gift of flight allowed her to use the sun's gravity to soar across the skies of Earth. Sirocco came from Italy and could control the winds, gliding effortlessly on wings crafted for him by Warlord.

And while this was occurring, they were still trying to sort out what had happened when the Fortunates attempted to land on Earth. The same could be said for the situation back on Mars, as they were hastily searching for answers to determine how to proceed with the extinction of earthlings and rid the universe of impure blood once and for all.

Experiments were conducted primarily on the transplanted earthlings residing within the dome of Ecopolis. While they were considered the purest of those who existed on Terra, traces of impure blood remained, making them worth sacrificing compared to the true purity of the Fortunates. This was all done in secrecy, with Magnus overseeing the progress of the chief scientist and his assistants.

In some ways, Luther thought this was a method to keep Magnus's aggression to a minimum and place him in a role of importance, as he constantly called for the use of the Guardians and even showed Luther where the detonation button was, emphasizing how simple it would be to activate the Guardians, which could only be described at the time as nuclear weapons, and lay waste to Earth once and for all. However, Luther also had another theory on why the experiments were confined to Ecopolis: they didn't want to put any of the Fortunates in harm's way if the experiments caused contamination, preferring to keep as far away from that risk as possible.

While there were small outbreaks of illness, they were kept to a minimum by eliminating the source. This was all done for the greater good, even if it meant the extermination of an individual.

The Apostles I

The Earth had given those who survived The Day of Decimation a gift—the hope to survive. This gift manifested as a mutated reaction of cells that, in some cases, granted extraordinary powers. The individuals most gifted with these abilities were known as the Apostles.

They assumed nicknames and appeared like superheroes from what Old Earth called comic books. While some may know their real names, the majority do not; they became immortalized by their heroic names. Although Apostles was initially just a nickname used by everyone, it would eventually become synonymous with them. No one knows for sure who first called them this, though Zachary Damir claims it was him. He exclaimed that if people were going to use the cognomen of the Pope for him simply because he now occupied the Fort Vatican, then these must be the twelve apostles, somewhat consistent with the Bible's account, as there was indeed a dozen of them. However, that statement was never recorded in any of the scrolls, so we cannot claim it as fact.

A formal introduction was staged near the crater intended to destroy Earth and all who lived on its soil. While all sources seem to reference the Christian Bible, most of the Apostles did not come from a religious background; it was merely a point of time and reference. As the Infidels were known for holding onto their historical values before the Fortunates' arrival, such as the old Julian calendar, this context is essential.

We refer to them as Apostles I, yet individuals prior to them in the Bible were also known as apostles. The current usage is purely for distinction, as another group during the Great War would later be referred to as Apostles II. This is not meant to disrespect those who still hold the Bible dear. While there is no direct correlation between the individuals now occupying the Vatican and its religious beginnings, they sometimes carry-on traditional names—probably more for relatability and familiarity.

The twelve individuals consisted of Granite, a large man made of solid stone. His size was thought to be due to his original human form being encased in stone. Sonic could blast sound extracted from his vocal cords, capable of puncturing walls if necessary. Sirocco had the power to control the winds, which many thought was vain, as he would sometimes command the wind simply to make his long, flowing hair blow back. The Omniscient One was granted the ability to see all that happened before her, along with glimpses of mind manipulation, though she had lost her sight as a young girl. This made her gift fascinating; unable to see with her eyes as others do, her vivid

memories of the past felt as though Earth had empowered her on that day to restore what had been taken away so many years ago.

Ra, a beautiful young girl, drew power from the sun, making her love for lying in it all day fitting. Link could be described as something between man and beast; if not for his status as an Apostle, the average person would likely fear him. Cullum possessed a somewhat ironic power; with the mere touch of his hands, he could break down molecules but was unable to rebuild his own. He appeared as a black mass, constantly breaking down and rebuilding, resembling the shape of a man but not fully appearing as one—almost like a shadow of himself.

What more can be said about the two sisters, Brevity and Entity? One could take life away, while the other could give life even to inanimate objects and, in some cases, small creatures like butterflies and insects, bringing them back to life. Given time, she might have been able to expand on that gift, but we will never know. Then there was Traverse, who had mastered the art of teleportation—something even Fortunates technology could not accomplish. While people referred to Regen as a form of teleportation, it was not in the truest sense, as it involved technology cloning cells.

Maniackal was a living, breathing organic machine, with limbs extending into either piercing metal or actual automatic weapons. He was unable to speak and could only be understood by one person, Warlord. Although he was viewed as the leader of the Apostles, he was never officially named. What he provided to the people of Earth would be far greater than what was known at the time. He could build and reconstruct metals into machinery at mere thought, relating to them as if they were his creations, almost as if he could not believe they were merely pieces of metal, as others would perceive them. Perhaps that is why he was able to understand Maniackal; he was practically a living machine himself. If not for an actual heart, many would consider him just a creation of Warlord's mind.

While all were granted these fantastic abilities, the ability to sacrifice was the greatest of all. They were true superheroes in every sense and, in some ways, Mother Earth's protectors. They should never be forgotten and most likely won't be, but they may eventually be regarded more as myth than as actual living beings.

The discovery was eventually made, and the theory was proven true: the Earth was rejecting the Martian blood and body makeup of the Fortunates. Moreover, the increased purity of Earthlings' blood would either remain unaffected or, in the case of the remaining Earthlings, result in a DNA reconstruction that mutated and granted its host a superior gene. Thus, despite the scientific advancements provided by the Fortunates over the years, including their genius in micro-biotic cells reproducing damaged ones and making them nearly immortal, nature took its course. A world that was once dying now had its spawn surviving —and thriving— with these mutations.

The beings of Earth also drew the same conclusion. Once the mightiest among them were assembled, an unveiling of their own became a cause for celebration. Just outside the great crater, a gathering was organized, and the protectors of their homeland were inaugurated as the Apostles, introduced to the world. With the Guardians still monitoring all happenings on Terra and projecting images back to Tropaion and the throne room in the golden tower, the Fortunates witnessed it too.

Adorned in unique outfits, twelve of Earth's new paladins stood before everyone. They assumed code names, as their given names would eventually be lost through time. It was their chosen names that would be remembered forever: Warlord, Granite, Maniackal, Sonic, Sirocco, Omniscient, Ra, Link, Cullum, Traverse, and the sisters Brevity and Entity. They stood before the crowd, aware that while people cheered in jubilation, those on Mars would have cause for concern. This realization brought smiles to each of their faces.

Training intensified as they knew the Fortunates would strike at some point; Earth was gaining in confidence and stability. The land was being restored, perhaps stronger than ever before. It was noted in the scrolls that one of the great empires had been restored, but this time, the boundaries drawn were based on the inner feeling that this was the land that was alive. If the heart of the planet was located in the old Middle East region, then the brain would keep it alive.

Desperate moves were now being initiated back on Mars. The Fortunates' confidence was suddenly struck by doubt—their fear that they would never be able to eradicate the impurity that populated the universe. It was their own doing, though, and Icon recognized that. A saying can be placed here: *What does not kill me makes me stronger*. At this moment, it could not be truer.

While many still referred to the area as Acre, the settlement now appeared more like the Roman Empire. This thought alone gave the Fortunates an unsettling feeling. Perhaps it was because of the old power of the empire, or maybe it was simply recognizable due to its location. No matter how much the Fortunates tried, they could not erase Earth's history, and it appeared that history would repeat itself—which would not bode well for the Fortunates.

With an order given, Ares was instructed to attack.

A GUARDIAN DIES

It was a day like any other, they said. The earthlings had proceeded with their regular order of business. The Apostles trained while the people braced for something to come their way—and on this day, it would. With an echo heard throughout the skies came the threat they had feared. The Apostles, however, felt otherwise. They took to the top of the Vatican and prepared for the confrontation to come.

Arrow Fighters floated out of Ares as it closed in, and when it crashed down to Earth, dozens of battalion soldiers raced out towards the gates. The new heroes of Earth were more than prepared. As waves of soldiers blasted their way forward, firing in every direction, the Apostles demonstrated what they had trained for. The Battalion was destroyed by winds summoned by Sirocco. Ra burned the off-balanced soldiers and melted the shells of the robotic army. Though sky attacks by the Arrows managed to strike the Vatican's walls, that was all they would accomplish, as Warlord controlled any machinery with the wave of his hands. He crushed the Arrows right in the sky, bringing them

to crash down on Earth's soil. Whether in hand-to-hand combat with the likes of Link and Granite, what became painfully obvious to the neighboring planet was that their Battalion soldiers were no match for the Apostles. The Battalion would now only be used as pawns to be sacrificed, merely buying time for whatever other combat the Fortunates might have in store. Ares then made its way towards the walls of the Vatican. As the lumbering giant approached, all of the Apostles focused on it, and what their advisories witnessed from so many miles away was more concerning than the quick defeat of the Battalion soldiers.

A well-coordinated strike on the massive machine ensued. The Apostles broke into teams and struck each limb of the behemoth. Being both slow and awkward in its maneuvering, as it took teams to coordinate all of Ares' functioning parts, the Guardian proved vulnerable. While the Guardians were an intimidating force as they hovered in space looking over Terra, they were not meant for hand-to-hand combat such as what Ares now faced. At the time of its construction, there had been no beings known as the Apostles.

The masses watched as Link, Maniackal and Granite kept any remaining Battalion soldiers at bay while the others continued their attacks on Ares. Its rockets and weaponry seemed futile against the Apostles, so it directed them at the Vatican instead, attempting to damage the structure that symbolized Earth's defiance.

Ra and Sonic blasted each extremity repeatedly from a distance—Ra with rays as powerful as the sun, and Sonic with direct impacts of piercing sound that struck like spears, puncturing Ares' armor with pinpoint accuracy. When close enough, Cullum broke down the molecules of Ares' feet, causing it to become unstable and eventually immobile. Sirocco commanded the winds to push the mighty Ares over, and it came crashing to the ground just outside the Vatican. Traverse teleported himself and Warlord right into Ares' command station, where Warlord crushed its remaining functions before the eyes of three Fortunates trying to maintain what life Ares had left. It was to no avail as Earth's atmosphere seeped in through all the punctures, dooming the Martian blooded Fortunates.

The massive warrior space station Guardian lay dormant, and all of the Apostles looked to the skies as if challenging the others that remained watching over Earth to come and suffer the same fate as the green war machine Ares had.

This caused a ripple effect back on Mars as it was told to us by Luther. The sheer panic that ensued was felt throughout. It was somewhat disbelief, but he stated that it was more than that. It was almost as if the Fortunates had seen this before. The confidence that they seemingly had for all their time spent on Terra seemed to disappear on that very day.

Both Icon and Agatha were infuriated and all that was known from what others had said is that Agatha kept referring to Bacchus and that she would not suffer the same fate as her father had.

Though the transplanted earthlings now living on Mars only received a somewhat edited version of what was going on. So, once again it was Magnus's voice that would be needed to settle the so-called rumors down and once again as he had to do back on earth, lie to the people and keep them in the dark. A belief that there would not be any sort of uprising as there had been back on the land he once commanded back on earth due to the population being so much less and the amount of Fortunates that had come through Goliath had now exceeded that of the former earthlings count that it would not be wise for anyone to attempt a rise such as the Infidels. But Magnus was taking no chances at this pivotal time and made sure the 13th Legion was well placed for any situation that may occur.

He did however wonder how the Martians were so privy to any information at all and just as Luther had put it out of his mind that Magnus would be part of a people that would see him commit genocide so too would Magnus relinquish thoughts of his brother being part of jeopardizing all that he had gained in the ranks of the Fortunates, but skepticism did exist. While power can make you an idol, power can also cause paranoia. Though, as we would find out during a period of war, Magnus's paranoia was not unfounded. From his actions he must have continued to sort through all possible scenarios as his actions would confirm. There was a crack in the dam and information was leaking through it. He was even suspecting individuals in the Court of Icon. Subtle suggestions would be made to both Icon and Agatha, but these suggestions were said to have them both begin to suspect Magnus. Was he too full of power and thirsting for more? A lesson in paranoia for all.

AGGRESSIVE BE THE ROYALS

Meetings were constant. Strategic planning was constant. The sound of agreeing and debating echoed throughout the Golden Tower. What had once been a beacon of strength upon its arrival not so long ago—both its halls and individuals alike—was no longer as powerful as it had recently seemed. And so began the Fortunates' aggressive planning. They would not suffer what Agatha had alluded to, and they would not run again. This was their land, their solar system, and as they saw it, their universe—but one thing at a time, Icon would urge. For now, all their attention would be paid to eliminating the population of their neighboring planet, Terra.

Because Icon no longer trusted many, constant closed-door meetings were set in place. We do not know the specifics of what occurred during those meetings; we can only speculate from the results of what happened next. How many failed ideas, intensive arguments, and debates had proceeded.

The closed doors always included Adom, Ajax and Echo and of course the Chief of science now known as Peripheral. Others were ushered in and out, but Magnus and Luther were almost always excluded.

The first strike would be to send Hades to the surface of Terra and begin to appear as though it would be attacking Jacob and his wall. This time there would be an unleashing and sacrifice of the Battalion army—and an army it would be. Tundra would crash the surface and release the soldiers, knowing full well that the Apostles would be there in an instant. With so many soldiers, most of the Apostles would have their time taken up disposing of them, and with that, the plan would be to draw out Warlord and capture him alone. From monitoring their training, they would attempt the same maneuvering as used to destroy Ares.

Apollo would then be dispatched toward the Vatican, but for nothing more than to have Traverse bring a portion of the Apostles to do battle with Apollo now that Warlord was seemingly prepared to gain control of

Hades just as he had with Ares. Warlord would enter the command center of Hades, but this time the fierce Endicots awaited, not just Battalion soldiers or average Fortunates. Using their Vitality Swords and looking to just subdue him rather than kill, they would incapacitate him, for they needed his brain alive to execute the next phase of their plan.

It worked to perfection, and when the Apostles saw Apollo retreat immediately, they knew it was just a diversion, but their recognition came too late. Warlord was captured and brought to Earth's moon where an Eco Pod called Mimas waited with Endicots lined throughout, prepared for any unforeseen attack. Mimas, while still an Eco Pod, did not appear in the usual hexagon shape but that of a dome, more like the Tune. None of the Battalion would be there for Warlord to manipulate and create weaponry from the machines as his power enabled him to do.

Hades would be gone before Warlord would come out of his sedated state, and before he could even know what was happening, Warlord was lobotomized by the waiting Fortunates, and his brain was extracted from his body. Still connected for

blood flow, it was placed in a device called ESP (Electrically Stimulated Procedure). Bacchians would tell us later that this art and apparatus was what was used for learning the art of Baccha.

With knowledge of the key chambers within the brain, they were now able to function the remaining Guardians from a distance, and the war machines became quicker to react and maneuver. They became more agile and thus more dangerous to the people of Earth. Step one of the Fortunates' plans had been completed. As referenced earlier, there were many layers to this plan, including the clandestine one that had begun long ago, but only now would it be escalated to its completion. Peripheral felt he had finally perfected it: the unveiling of the G.O.D.S. (Genetically Orchestrated Defense Squadron).

An unknown Fortunate named Kane entered the throne room with seven beings—six males and one female. All were outfitted in uniforms reminiscent of ninjas from the early days of old Earth. Kane did not appear like the other Fortunates. He instead possessed natural skin and flowing hair. By all accounts, he appeared like those of Earth, with a strong jaw and gripping features outlined by dark, flowing brown hair and piercing blue eyes. He eventually would be introduced to all of the Martians, but on this day, he was only to present the seven G.O.D.S. Four were fully masked, but two of the males had an outline around their mouths showing what appeared to be skin, and the female of the group had the same piercing blue eyes and surrounding skin showing through.

While they moved with the flexibility of humans, they were anything but human. They were super soldiers—they were androids. And if they were called G.O.D.S., it may have been Peripheral referring to himself.

Kane & The G.O.D.S

Among the many reasons people of Leviathan believed Fortunates walked among them, a major factor was the creation of the G.O.D.S. (Genetically Orchestrated Defense Squadron). While these soldiers carried Energy Swords similar to those wielded by the Endicots, their weapons were more elegant and lighter. In battle, the G.O.D.S. preferred using these weapons as swords rather than exploiting their full capabilities as firing arms.

The G.O.D.S. were created by Peripheral, one of the Chief Scientists among the Fortunates. His study of human anatomy began on Fortuna but reached perfection only after arriving in the Mars-Earth solar system. The crucial breakthrough was his mastery of skin cell development—something lost to the people of Fortuna since their advancement into micro-biotics. Some believed they had traded their anatomy for immortality.

While the progression toward his goal produced many achievements, the first model—aptly named One—was no less remarkable than the final model that would become known as Kane. These androids contained no living tissue; every component was manufactured and enhanced with accelerated micro-biotic technology capable of regenerating entire limbs.

When Peripheral successfully generated skin cells that perfectly simulated a functioning being, complete with natural movement and a voice box that replicated actual vocal cords, he unveiled Kane to all. Kane possessed full memories of a prior life and remained unaware that he wasn't a living, breathing being. He led the G.O.D.S. in battles, believing himself to be merely their instructor until he was chosen to lead the team on Terra's surface. He questioned how this was possible, knowing that all beings without high levels of earthling blood had perished when exposed to the planet's toxic atmosphere. Initially, he assumed he would be equipped with enhanced medications or a protective suit. When he noted that only machines had survived, the truth suddenly dawned on him.

Unless told otherwise, no one could distinguish Kane from a living being. His only obvious artificial feature was a bionic eye, which concealed a mechanism known only to Peripheral—an access panel to the android's artificial brain. Kane's perfection led many to believe that Adom had survived and that other High Fortunates remained hidden after the Golden Tower raid. These beliefs, combined with occasional scripture appearances throughout Leviathan, convinced many that they *traveled aboard the nomadic city, waiting to emerge if the vessel ever reached Fortuna.*

The G.O.D.S. were numbered One through Seven, with no names except for the female unit. The numbering likely reflected their order of creation and subsequent improvements. All were mute except for Seven, who could manage one-word sentences. It was Seven's ability to speak that led to naming the female unit "Lady," as that was how he referred to her. The most renowned among them were Lady, Seven, and their leader Kane. They carried slimmer versions of the Endicots' weapons, with Lady and Seven wielding two each. Enhanced with micro-biotic technology, they could regenerate lost limbs instantly. Kane proudly demonstrated their combat capabilities, claiming credit for their training.

Magnus and Luther attended their unveiling, marveling at these creations. The Fortunates then appointed Luther to accompany Kane and the G.O.D.S., along with Battalion fleets, to resume his position in Apollo. Whether this assignment stemmed from Kane's loyalty, Luther's knowledge of humans and Terra's landscape, or as a test of his commitment to the Fortunates remained unclear. Regardless, Luther returned to his role as general, tasked with coordinating the next assault on his former homeland.

Magnus also received a more prominent role beyond his position as liaison between the Fortunates and Martians. Due to information leaks, the 13th Legion was placed on high alert, with Battalion soldiers now patrolling Ecopolis daily. The Fortunates recognized Magnus's dissatisfaction with his handling of the Infidels' rise and knew he would seek redemption by ensuring the people of Mars would never contemplate such resistance again. They were confident in his willingness to enforce these measures.

The plan for annihilation moved forward, but Earth's inhabitants weren't idle during this period. They had learned that the Fortunates would persist until humanity's extinction. Both throne holders at the Vatican and Constantinople—understood this reality clearly. While Jacob favored a defensive mindset, Pope Damir focused on offensive strategies. Unlike the republic before them, there were no votes needed; both men pursued their goals independently while keeping each other informed, united in their common purpose: the survival of Earth's humanity.

Damir often kept his plans from the masses, not from fear of opposition but as a matter of character. When the metallic remnants of what was once known as Ares disappeared from outside the Vatican's gates, he claimed it was to create an unobstructed defensive perimeter. Later, it would become clear that the former Guardian's remains served a greater purpose. The Vatican had transformed, now bristling with warriors manning its walls and weaponry throughout. While Constantinople's wall appeared more intimidating, the Vatican had become the more formidable fortress.

The Apostles relocated from the Vatican to the former Tune. Though more dilapidated since the Day of Decimation, the building's deteriorated exterior belied its significance. Now known as "Apostles' Hall," its interior remained pristine under their occupation, transforming this former

symbol of Fortunate power outside Panspermia into their own stronghold.

Every earthling action served strategic warfare and defense purposes. They dispersed power centers and strongholds, developed rumored underground dwellings to evade surveillance from above, and created deliberate mock imagery to confuse their observers. The Fortunates struggled to distinguish between real earthling capabilities and deception, unsure of the full extent of their opponents' newfound powers.

Nevertheless, the Fortunates proceeded with their plans. Hades and the G.O.D.S. launched their attack. As Hades entered Earth's atmosphere, Apostles' Hall responded instantly, with Traverse teleporting the Apostles to the Vatican's gates.

Uncharacteristically, Pope Damir had withheld information about a new addition to their defensive force. Racing from the Vatican's gates came Gravitas, filling the void left by Warlord. Though Gravitas's full story would unfold in the coming war, for now, he served simply as one of their own.

The G.O.D.S. engaged the Apostles in a battle that defied description. They fought both individually and as a coordinated unit, but the Apostles held firm in defending their capital. Meanwhile, Hades departed toward Constantinople, intent on breaching its walls and destroying all written records. The Fortunates aimed to erase Earth's very existence from universal memory, along with its heroes and the damage they had inflicted upon it.

Traverse transported Sonic, Sirocco, Entity, and—at Zachary's insistence—Gravitas to Constantinople. From Apollo, Luther and Kane monitored the battle below, waiting for the perfect moment to deploy their Arrow Fighters. Hades, now controlled remotely by ESP from the moon and Mimas, moved with unexpected agility. It set the ground ablaze while advancing like the devil himself, hurling boulder sized bombs at the massive wall.

Sonic's usually precise attacks proved less effective against the nimbler Hades, unlike their success against the stationary Ares. As Hades rapidly approached the wall, Jacob emerged to join the battle, following in his father's footsteps. He manipulated the land, creating craters to impede Hades' advance.

While Traverse secretly relocated the historical archives beneath Constantinople, Jacob continued holding off Hades, destabilizing the ground beneath the scarlet Guardian. He succeeded in nearly halting its progress, standing at the edge of a massive crater, satisfied that he had thwarted the Fortunates' objective.

However, Gravitas's intervention proved catastrophic. Using his power to manipulate gravity on any surface he touched, he laid his hands on the ground where Jacob had created the crater. Whether from inexperience, lack of control, or battle excitement, his action created an enormous hole reaching the lower mantle. While it appeared to send Hades plummeting to hell, Jacob, standing too close to the crater's edge, lost his footing. As Hades made one final grasp at the crater's edge, both it and Jacob fell into the molten lava below.

Jubilation instantly transformed into shock. Jacob had met the same fate as his father, dying in battle and immortalizing the DeLuca legacy. The remaining Apostles quickly regrouped, as the battle outside the Vatican still raged on, and Traverse needed to return them there despite the tragic loss.

Though neither side suffered additional casualties, the G.O.D.S. proved formidable opponents against the Apostles. Their regenerating cells made them nearly indestructible, but when reinforcements arrived, Kane requested Luther to deploy the Arrows and extract his team. The three-person Arrow Fighters operated with two Battalion soldiers, leaving the third seat for each of the seven they retrieved.

The battle ended in stalemate. Only two Guardians remained, and only the Vatican's throne remained occupied. Constantinople's seat stood empty as the earthlings consolidated their forces between the Vatican and Apostles' Hall.

Zachary, with a clenched fist slamming the stone table, swore revenge. Though Gravitas received forgiveness, he would not participate in the next mission. Pope Damir blamed himself for not properly integrating Gravitas into the Apostles' training beforehand—a mistake he vowed never to repeat.

Then came what many earthlings claimed was Jacob's voice, speaking after being consumed with Hades deep within the planet. Given the now known strength of the bond between all, perhaps it was true. His words were recorded in the scrolls as quotes rather than mere scripture:

"Do not mourn my death, for I will be dining and drinking with my father from this day forward. You must press on and make our lives mean something, my brothers and sisters, for mother earth has given us a chance to protect her and, more importantly, to live on as her children."

The Fortunates shared in the remorse, not for the loss of Hades itself, but for the destruction of another defensive machine—a development that Icon had feared.

<u>ATTACK ON MIMAS</u>

In the days following, Zachary Damir ensured everyone remained focused on his plan of action. He revealed it gradually—not from fear of betrayal among the Earthlings, but because he knew they were under constant surveillance. And indeed, they were.

Luther maintained his position in Apollo while the G.O.D.S. returned home, leaving only Kane behind. Whether Luther had devised the next course of action independently or misinterpreted Zachary's intentions, his actions served their purpose. Luther claimed he had witnessed Zachary's planning and took it upon himself to feed Magnus different information, ultimately giving Pope Damir's true plan a better chance of success.

Luther informed Magnus that they planned to attack Goliath, aiming to disable the portal to Fortuna and prevent more Fortunates from joining the already substantial population on Mars. When Magnus relayed this information to Icon and the others, it reinforced both his and Luther's loyalty to the Fortunates. Luther was ordered to defend the gateway with Apollo, supported by Battalion fleets and numerous ships. The scale of defense suggested a greater threat than publicly known—as would later become apparent. Now only Zeus stood between the two neighboring planets, a detail that would prove significant.

Luther's claim gained credibility when the Pope unveiled a new vessel more heavily armed than their shuttles. Named Tiburon, it rose from beneath the waters near Apostles Hall, its sleek, smooth exterior gleaming bright against the dome's dark facade. The control cabin windows lined its belly like teeth ready to strike, its shape and stature resembling a selachimorpha—commonly known as a shark.

The true plan was revealed only to those directly involved. The eleven Apostles flew to the Vatican, where each step was planned, executed, and immediately destroyed, with Omniscient One retaining the information through her power to see the past. This prevented their opposition from witnessing or hearing their true intentions.

Icon and the Fortunates, confident in their intelligence, allowed arrogance to fill the Golden Tower within Tropaion's dome. Their primary concern remained Goliath's defense, with Icon and Agatha's preoccupation with the bridge evident to all. Luther and Kane oversaw vessel passage, though Luther found the thorough searching of incoming ships peculiar. The relieved expressions of arriving Fortunates suggested untold stories from the other side of the bridge.

The Apostles trained rigorously, determined to succeed. When the time came, they boarded Tiburon, each receiving a farewell embrace from Zachary. They understood this might be a one-way mission but recognized its necessity.

Meanwhile, Magnus urged using Zeus as the weapon it was, capable of destroying Terra once and for all. Icon's reluctance and Agatha's cryptic warning that Zeus's preservation was crucial for an unnamed future purpose added to the mounting questions about what lay beyond Goliath.

As Tiburon ascended toward space, Zeus moved to intercept its apparent path to Goliath. The defending forces prepared for battle, marking Earth's first offensive since the famous "Battle of Gibraltar" and "Seizing of the Tune." The Fortunates watched from Mars as a second ship—a shuttle carrying only Clone—followed behind.

The true target revealed itself when Tiburon suddenly changed course toward Earth's moon. Their objective wasn't Goliath but ESP and the Fortunates residing within Mimas. Zeus received urgent orders to intercept while others could only watch, too distant to assist.

Traverse teleported the Apostles into Mimas's Eco Pod, where they initially faced only a small force of Endicots and Battalion soldiers. As they searched for ESP and Warlord's dormant body, they easily overcame the initial resistance. However, this defense bought crucial time for Zeus's arrival.

When Zeus crashed through the dome, exposing the Apostles to the moon's atmosphere, they were prepared with atmospheric helmets and weighted boots—technology left behind by the Fortunates in the Tune. Yet their powers proved limited in space: Sonic's blasts weakened, Sirocco's wind abilities diminished, and Ra's solar power waned. The battle fell primarily to Ra, Cullum, and Entity.

As Traverse searched for ESP, Apostles fell one by one. Entity, the last standing, animated a building to restrain Zeus while Traverse retrieved Brevity—Entity's sister with the power to take life. Brevity eliminated the

Fortunates protecting ESP while Traverse attempted to evacuate their survivors. In a final confrontation, a surviving Fortunate scientist commanded Zeus to strike down the remaining Apostles just as Brevity drained the last life from Warlord's body.

The mission succeeded at a terrible cost. Zeus became inoperable, and Clone, waiting in the shuttle, replicated himself to pilot both vessels back to Earth. Icon and Agatha furiously dispatched Tundra to repopulate Zeus with Battalion and Endicots, though the Guardian would never regain its former power.

Luther again faced scrutiny, summoned to defend himself before the Fortunates in the Golden Tower's court. On Earth, while Tiburon stood as a reminder of their losses, Clone received a hero's welcome at the Vatican. Pope Damir and Cornelius acknowledged his success with solemn appreciation, knowing more phases of Zachary's plan lay ahead. The statues eventually erected atop Fort Vatican would forever honor their fallen heroes and those yet to come.

THE TRIAL OF LUTHER CARTER

These are the words of Luther Carter as he told them. As he stood in the court before all the known and significant Fortunates, Luther thought his life would end that day.

While Magnus was present, he was only there as a witness to the trial. Seated before him were both Icon and Agatha, along with Adom, Ajax, Peripheral, and Echo. The trial, as Icon had explained from the start, would be brief—which to Luther implied a predetermined outcome.

Luther brought support for his findings, presenting why he believed the attack would target Goliath instead of the moon of Terra. His evidence was extensive and precise. Either he had manipulated all the data to his advantage, or he was telling the truth.

One wonders if this was a deliberate ploy by Zachary Damir to create a diversion or if there had been another objective, perhaps a course of action abandoned after observing the Fortunates' movements. We may never know, for Zachary is no longer alive, and the answers he once gave were vague. Although Cornelius likely knew the same truths, his constant response remained, *Time changes everything. Zachary is gone now, let him rest.*

Luther continued to argue that he acted solely on the information he had gathered, insisting that his loyalty lay with the Fortunates. He reminded the court that the pure Martian blood running through his veins had guided his decisions.

Whether Adom felt personally responsible for choosing Luther or simply recognized that the facts supported his actions remains unclear. Ultimately, it was the Fortunates' decision, not Luther's alone, to remove Apollo from its station in Terra's outer atmosphere.

They could have repositioned Apollo, as they did with Zeus, to align with Goliath and bolster its defenses. In that case, Apollo could have followed Zeus's example and been ready to

assist. Perhaps Adom sympathized with Luther's situation, knowing firsthand the burden of being a messenger.

Luther was escorted out of the room alongside Magnus as the remaining leaders deliberated his fate. The discussion dragged on for hours— whether to induce anxiety or because the debate was genuine, Luther could not tell.

When he was called back in, they informed him that the vote had been four to two. However, they did not disclose the alternative action or who cast the dissenting votes. In the end, Luther was allowed to keep his position among the Fortunates. He would return to Apollo to guard Goliath's gateway, accompanied by Peripheral, while also training Kane in entry protocols and warfare tactics.

Though Luther avoided the punishment he had feared, he claimed that something inside him died that day—and a different man was born in his place.

It was also at that moment that everyone noticed the strain between the two brothers. While Magnus appeared genuinely relieved by the outcome and supportive of Luther, a fracture in their trust had formed. Luther believed that Magnus must have aligned with the Fortunates to some extent—otherwise, why had Magnus not faced trial as well?

Even though Magnus remained supportive during the trial, Luther couldn't help but wonder if he had been manipulated. Had Magnus intentionally placed himself in a position to offer crucial information, knowing it could make him an outcast among Mars's leaders?

Luther reflected that blood alone does not determine loyalty. Loyalty stems from who you choose to be—and often, from the choices you make when it matters most. This is how you become you.

Tiburon

What began as only a glimmer of hope Tiburon soon became synonymous with heroism. This vessel not only served as the primary transport for the Apostles but also symbolized the human spirit's unyielding will to live and fight for survival.

Of all the awe-inspiring creations Warlord achieved before his untimely death, none rivaled the significance of Tiburon. Perhaps it was what the vessel represented to Earth's last survivors—a statement that humanity would protect itself and the world it called home.

With its sleek, silver design, Tiburon streaked across the skies of Earth, resembling a shooting star. But beneath that smooth exterior lay a formidable force, armed for battle.

ANTIQUITY

To its enemies, Tiburon was a terrifying opponent. It was no accident that the vessel, rising from the waters beneath Apostles Hall, took on the form of a shark from a side view. The cabin extended forward above the windows, which were set along the underbelly—resembling the teeth of a shark. In length, it was comparable to a passenger plane from Earth's earlier days, when humans traveled from city to city. Yet, from above, its wingspan evoked a sea creature—whole and expansive like a manta ray.

Warlord's mutated gift, bestowed upon him during the Day of Decimation, allowed him to reshape metal and weaponize it. This talent reached its peak in Tiburon, unmatched by any other creation. The vessel struck fear in its enemies and hope in its allies. Many fell victim to its might, and it became a symbol of resilience for those who survived.

RISE OF THE APOSTLES

If it wasn't war yet, it would soon be seen as one. Until the day the Pope ordered the strike on the moon, most of the conflict had been about defending themselves from extinction. But, just like Jacob, Zachary was not one to rest on his accomplishments. He was a man of action, understanding that an enemy would stop at nothing to ensure their elimination.

Zachary knew that the Fortunates didn't wish to coexist. Though he didn't fully understand the roots of their beliefs, he knew the outcome: total annihilation of their opposition. And he was determined to ensure that this future would not happen without a fight.

<u>*APOSTLES II*</u>

The last residents of Apostles Hall were known as the Apostles II. Although their predecessors were more legendary, these Apostles were just as essential to the battle on Mars. While the first Apostles were more disciplined and proper, this new group had one goal: eliminate the Fortunates. Time and experience had shifted their mentality from defense to eradication.

Among them was Gravitas, who had previously been involved in a most unfortunate situation. It was a disaster that neither he nor Zachary should have ever faced, but instead of dwelling on it, Gravitas returned to train with a new group—another strategic secret of Zachary's. Perhaps it was a morbid contingency plan, or maybe Zachary simply believed there should always be a new team waiting. It could also have been foresight, given the capture of the Warlord.

Just as he had done with Tiburon, Zachary only revealed his hidden weapon when necessary. This time, that weapon was the second wave of Apostles, following the loss of the originals on the moon. There was little celebration when they were introduced—perhaps because their emergence came at the cost of others' deaths, or maybe because these were darker days.

Nevertheless, the new Apostles were introduced:

- Gravitas could manipulate gravity by touch, controlling both the intensity and the area of effect. Over time, he also learned

to levitate slightly, something that had escaped him on the day Jacob fell. That day taught him that rigorous training was essential, and he eventually became the leader of the new Apostles.

- Radon harnessed radiation, increasing his strength and projecting bursts of energy toward his enemies.

- Contact grew in strength and mass through contact with any living thing, though he could not project that power outward.

- Core resembled molten lava from beneath the earth's surface; his touch melted anything in battle.

- Angel lived up to her name, possessing wings of light that allowed her to glide gracefully. But to cross her meant facing the burning sting of that same light.

- Terrain was a brute who could absorb the ground beneath his feet and hurl it at his enemies. His attacks varied depending on the type of terrain—an unpredictable and dangerous force.

-Dementia had the power to invade the minds of her enemies, planting disturbing images that could drive them to madness.

-Masquerade could mimic the appearance of any person she touched and, in some cases, even replicate a fraction of their abilities and memories.

-Darter bore a striking resemblance to one of the original Apostles, though he neither confirmed nor denied the connection. Half man, half beast, he teetered on the edge of control more wild than Link ever was.

-Fantasia could transform into light and move at light speed, though he avoided doing so since light can only travel in a straight line, limiting his aim.

- Asteroza had multiple limbs, and if any were severed, they would spawn new beings. These clones could later be reabsorbed into his body.

- Toxic manipulated gases, turning them into solid forms. It was rumored that he could become a gas himself, though he hesitated to try, fearing he might not reform correctly.

Together, these twelve Apostles were seen as Earth's last hope against the Fortunates. Though not all would survive the final battle on Mars, they found solace in the knowledge that only one Apostle was lost—and that his sacrifice would be remembered as heroic.

Though Zachary mourned the loss of the fallen Apostles, he recognized the significance of their accomplishment. The Fortunates, once seen as unbeatable, were now forced to divide their forces between defending their stronghold on Mars and Goliath. Merely forcing the Fortunates into a defensive position was a victory in itself. They were no longer invincible—still formidable, but now relying on their superior technology and numbers.

Earth had managed to level the playing field, using every gift and resource available. And Zachary would make sure those gifts were used to their fullest potential.

Beneath the Vatican, a clandestine operation was unfolding. The Pope's next move was not just a show of strength—it was a statement of intent. On a day dedicated to honoring the fallen Apostles, Zachary and Cornelius addressed a crowd gathered in the heart of the Vatican.

As they paid tribute to the original Apostles, statues of each hero were unveiled, standing atop the walls of the Vatican, alongside its artillery. Zachary concluded his speech with powerful words:

They are not, and will never be, replaced but they will be joined by the next wave of defenders!

At that moment, twelve individuals stepped through the grand doors and joined Zachary and Cornelius. The intimidating new Apostles stood before the crowd, their faces marked by determination and anger. Unlike their predecessors, who were greeted with celebration, these Apostles seemed to carry the weight of their mission on their shoulders.

Watching from Mars through surveillance systems, Icon and the Fortunates could not hide their concern as they saw the new Apostles: Gravitas, Radon, Contact, Core, Terrain, Angel, Dementia, Masquerade, Darter, Fantasia, Asteroza, and Toxic. Even Agatha was said to have whispered, almost in tears, *It feels as though the world of Bacchus is everywhere.*

The Apostles gazed out at the crowd and then toward the stars. The people sensed it—a war was coming. Not today, not tomorrow, but soon.

The next few months saw the Fortunates increase their production and prepare for conflict, all while keeping a close watch on their homeland on Mars. War is never spontaneous—it is built upon a series of events, waiting for the right moment to erupt.

On Earth, constant planning was underway. There could be no mistakes, no room for error. A great leader anticipates every outcome—and that's who Zachary Damir was. He fought for Earth, but his true motivation was the preservation of his people.

The only problem? Icon was driven by the same desire.

EVERYTHING HAPPENS AS IT SHOULD

If you look back on every moment and realize that one moment cannot exist without all the others that came before, you understand: you are exactly where you are supposed to be. Whether the universe has a calling for you or the script has already been written, the final act can only play out if every role is performed as intended. And though everything leading to this moment for Luther had contributed to his being here, none was more significant than the day he stared into the abyss of the haze through Goliath—undoubtedly wondering what lay beyond and what the Fortunates were hiding.

It was on that day that he found his answer. A voice spoke inside his mind. In that moment, his part in the grand design became clear, and the universe summoned him to act.

Luther described it as similar to the arrival of Adom, but more natural—fluent. Though it was a cry for help, it carried a sense of peace. He didn't second guess it, despite knowing he was being closely watched. He knew without question that he had to do this.

He realized that, while the Fortunates had granted him a position of prominence, offering power and control, they had never let him forget that he was under their command. As a military man, Luther respected the chain of command, but this was different. The Fortunates used him as a pawn in a larger game of chess, where the king was hidden, and a knight could strike him down at any moment.

No hesitation. Something inside him recognized this as a turning point what he was destined to do. He vowed that neither Kane nor Peripheral would witness his actions, and even if they realized what he had done, it would be too late. He would ensure that by the time they noticed, he had already reached the point of no return.

This story comes directly from Luther, so there are no other accounts to confirm it. But what he described aligns with what others experienced that day—or at least with the outcome.

Luther said it felt like divine intervention, as if he were watching someone else carry out the act, yet knowing it was him. He completed everything as if it were preordained, each moment aligning exactly as his mind had told him it would. He even questioned whether the guiding voice in his mind was his true self, and his body merely a shell carrying out the script.

At just the right moment, Kane and Peripheral were distracted long enough for Luther to allow the voice's request. By the time Kane noticed the portal had been opened, it was too late. Kane rushed to retrieve Peripheral and reported Luther's actions, but the log only showed that a portal had been activated—it showed no signs of any vessel passing through.

The log wasn't wrong. Something had come through, but not a vessel in the traditional sense. What entered was organic alive. The scanners couldn't register it as anything recognizable. But Luther knew, deep down, that something had passed through. He didn't know what it was, but he knew that opening the way had been just and right.

The Bacchians had entered the Copernicus system, and everything was about to change.

At that moment, Luther turned to Kane. Kane later recounted Luther's words, saying they sent chills down his spine:

War is inevitable when both sides believe they are justified. It's not land they seek, it's the island of righteousness they stand on. Better to unleash the wrath of war upon the people now. There can be no peaceful resolution, my dear Kane.

War would soon spread across the neighboring planets, a destiny written in the stars ages ago.

Zachary Damir made it clear that the Fortunates wanted nothing less than the destruction of Earth, refusing to coexist as separate kingdoms in peace. After delivering a rousing speech that galvanized the Earthlings to rally together, it became clear: Earth was no longer on the defensive. They were prepared to strike back and end the struggle once and for all.

His final words on that day were recorded, his voice booming with conviction:

If it's genocide the Fortunates want, then genocide they will receive!

REVELATIONS OF WAR

<u>VOX INTUS</u>

Luther's words resonated on both planets now. His words were not meant to be a cry out to either side, it was just as he had seen it. He would tell no one of the voices that had entered his head. With the knowledge gained by the Fortunates by way of Kane of what Luther had done, he was ordered back to Mars. Once again, he found himself needing to defend his actions, to which he claimed there were no actions taken. It was just a mistake, and the logs had shown that nothing had entered during that momentary opening.

The people of Mars described Luther as more confident this time. Though, he would tell us that it was because he had felt an inner being or force driving his actions. This script was written, and he was accepting whatever might happen to him. Just as Peter had claimed at one time, and others from the region, they were fighting for their preservation—that it was something far greater than their understanding. It was as though the universe or something in their deep-seeded past had entered their subconscious, and they knew what needed to be done because it was in their DNA to do so.

An inherent past that had created and made them who they were all along.

When Luther finally did enter the chambers where Icon and Agatha waited on him, they both sensed Luther's conviction too. Luther would tell us that it even prompted Adom to ask,

"What do you know, Luther?"

And he said he answered it as honestly as he could.

"I know everything, yet nothing at all"

He stated that while Adom was perplexed by the wording, he didn't seem as bewildered at the feeling he was trying to delineate. And then he expressed to Luther a quote that was shared by an author of Earth, to which he said:

"We can only know that what we know is nothing. And that is the highest degree of Wisdom."

If there was one thing that the Fortunates did bring to us all, it was a greater understanding of the stars and the impact that the universe had on all of us. With this understanding, Icon and all others in the room seemed worried towards Luther's words at first, but then he said he searched their faces for more and suddenly he understood that it was actually fear.

And with that Luther was released. It was as though the Fortunates feared that had punishment been more severe, it would have set his place in the history books as a martyr, or it would have stimulated a movement amongst those now residing on Mars. We must remember that the Fortunates are a people that have had a great respect for their history and to not allow it to repeat itself. Along with that, they are also a people that want to see all others' history abolished and that only their version matters. It is why they truncated their release of history as to who they were and why they had left. They were hoping to have the people of Earth not look into it any further. For inquisitive minds stimulate questions, and questions inspire answers, and answers result in one gaining knowledge. Thus, becoming a mind that is less easy to manipulate. It is why they felt so threatened by the Omniscient One, which had the capability to reach within her memory

and witness so much more than she had time to reveal to others before her life was taken away from her.

There is an inner you that we must always recall. The days of the past are constantly calling to us and if we do not listen to it, we have no way of defending ourselves from it occurring again. The alignment of the stars can only place us in the right position to make these decisions; it is what you do at that moment with the opportunities that were presented to you that can impact the timeline one way or the other. And if you are not maintaining all the information given to you in the past, you may not be capable of not repeating an errant way.

The choice of the Fortunates would end up being wrong, but that too can only be said if you believe that a story has an ending—most do not. And for that reason, it is believed that the Fortunates would allow Luther to just walk away. Something in their history made them believe that this was the right course of action. But a very cautious eye would be kept on him.

And during this time Luther had waited for either his own voice to speak to him or from the one that requested his help, but either way he knew there would be another calling.

LUTHER'S CALLING

Some would believe that the most significant happening was the day Luther heard the voice again, but it would be unbeknownst to most at the time. Others believed that this was a war already and this was just another moment in the building block of events.

The voice called. This time it was his name that came across and it was not a plea but an engaging voice that appeared to be offering help as opposed to asking for it. A conversation ensued, but only within the mind. The voice introduced himself. His name was Darrd and claimed to be a Fortunate that now lived on the planet of Bacchus. The voice continued to explain that he and what he called the Acolytes were here to help. They were currently resting beneath the thick clouds of Jupiter but needed to get closer if they were going to assist in the war that was coming. He continued to explain that a war was already raging on the other side of the portal. A story that dated back to the arrival of the Martians. And he was all too familiar with the actions of the now known Fortunates.

Darrd expressed that there was a total of seven Acolytes plus himself, but one would nest on Vesta, one of the largest meteors in the asteroid belt which also included a story of days past but would be left for another time.

The Fortunates see themselves as superior to all other known species throughout the galaxy and will stop at nothing to cleanse the universe of impurity. They believe it is their purpose, and the theory was not born with Icon or Agatha—it had been going on through multiple turns in the stars.

Darrd then urged Luther to seek a way for he and the Acolytes to gain access to Mars so that they can help. It was at that time that he urged Luther to somehow reach out to the people of Earth and let them know to not act hastily and wait upon their arrival.

Luther knew he would play a part in this war that was unfolding the day he let the Bacchians through, but he did not know to what extent. His life had all led to this moment just as all of us have encountered a pivotal moment in life. Again, there are some more recognizable than others but each experience leads to the next and without the other then you cannot be where you are supposed to be. And Luther's path of decisions and experiences had led him to this one. The universe or what was perceived as God has a strange way of working but in the end if not for every one of those preceding decisions, chance meetings, failures you would not be able to do what is needed to be done and Luther was about to choose the one he was meant to.

Being a general alongside his brother throughout Ecopolis he knew the landscape very well. That landscape even included the restricted tunnels that were being built for possible irrigation or just mining for minerals and at some lengths a possible finding of ancient artifacts that may have shown the existence of the Fortunates residing on Mars. But all of those reasons meant nothing at this point in time and the only thing of concern to Luther. Since all that transpired it had since been abandoned and left for a more settling time. The entrance to the tunnel lay at the furthest point of Ecopolis and well off the ways from the dome that housed Tropaion and also the section that saw itself grounded between Tropaion and Ecopolis known as Endicots Lair.

The next thing would be passing the Acolytes through any patrols that the Fortunates had set in place. With heightened security this would be the most challenging task. He watched and he waited carefully, surveying any sort of consistencies that were taking place. Panspermia was the largest of these obstacles and as fortune would have it, it was fixated on the path from Earth to Mars. And most of the comings and goings of any Arrow Fighters did not venture very far from Panspermia. With the Acolytes currently positioned on Jupiter it would only need to await an alignment of the planets so that exposure to any entry would have all of the Fortunates focusing on the direction of the sun.

Luther began meeting up with Magnus again on a regular basis and though Magnus thought it to be a bit peculiar he accepted that his brother was reaching out to him. Magnus believed or at least wanted to believe that his brother never acted with intent and that all of the events that unfolded were truly accidental and that Luther had placed himself in unnecessary jeopardy by not embracing all that the Fortunates were doing. It is always good to remember that Magnus, very much like the Fortunates, saw himself as superior to most and that was long before their arrival.

In a time of war much of a person is revealed. In life it takes extreme situations for them to be exposed as to who they really are, and war is one of those times. And though Magnus and Luther share the same blood they are by no means the same souls.

A patience was set in order by Luther. He had much to set in place. One wrong step and everything would have gone awry. He needed to somehow get in touch with the people of Earth and let them know that help was coming and that they needed to wait before taking any action, but that would have to see them trusting him. While there were rumors of Luther's inconsistent behavior of late, they were not on Mars to truly witness it. They would not trust any of the Bacchians to contact them through the mind as they had only known of the Fortunates to have such a power and would probably think they

were being set for a trap. He also had to make sure that the Fortunates did not intercept any message.

So, it was decided that he would reach the people of Mars through a cryptic form of telecommunication to the new Martians by creating a voice from the underground called Veracity. A hooded individual that sent out information to the people about who the Fortunates were. At this point he did not have enough information himself, but he would release whatever he did know and by way of diverting the communication it appeared that the information was coming from the people of Earth. Transmissions were constantly blocked but enough words were released for the people of Mars to start questioning and for the people of Earth to hear that something was occurring. It was brief the infiltration, but it was enough to plant the seed of doubt along with now having Earth know that someone had gained more information than they were privy to. So, they waited and then Veracity disappeared.

It was also enough to have the Fortunates realize that the Bacchians were here or a person of power on Terra had begun gaining the knowledge of remembering. It was why they feared the Omniscient One, but she did not live long enough to see it all. Or the last option would be that there may be a traitor amongst them.

Of course, Luther was suspected but by way of technology he had released information when he was actually in the presence of Adom once and that was enough for the accusations to subside. They then turned their focus to Magnus, but that was quickly dispersed as Magnus had probably been more loyal to their cause than even some Fortunates themselves. So, they did begin to look inner, and the next step was interrogating their own. They began with the most recent arrivals and from what we know the interrogation was in some cases extreme.

It mattered not to the hierarchy of the Fortunates at this point as to what they were pursuing but more to the point was that they didn't have control of the situation, and if any Fortunates were to show disloyalty to the cause then it may impede on their greater plan in the future. It would also mean that the person capable of being disloyal is an act against their own and they couldn't have anyone not believing in what they were looking to achieve. Being sedulous on their own was of utmost importance and any other way of thinking would be considered treason.

Luther looked on and understood that there was so much more that he needed to know and wanted to know, but he had to keep himself from getting distracted and the next phase would be to get in touch with the Pope himself. Maybe it was one of those moments that the universe put everything in place again, but Luther was asked to head to Apollo once again and relieve Peripheral of his station being that all entry had been halted. He of course would not be there alone. Kane would accompany him but that allowed enough of an opportunity, as Kane was just one obstacle to overcome as opposed to the Fortunates being able to apply so many watchful eyes while being on Mars.

Apollo was a huge piece of machinery, as has been referenced so many times before, and it would be easy for Luther to lose himself for a brief time. Long enough to contact Zachary. He stated that he had just thought to himself, that he was concerned that the people of Earth hadn't already made any coordinated plans to initiate any formal attacks that would have the Fortunates retaliate before he was able to get Darrd and the Acolytes to Mars.

He had already stalled the Fortunates actions by having Veracity release information that made them wonder and have cause for concern in pursuing any action against Earth until they knew what they were up against. It wasn't his intent, but the cause and effect resulted in what would be advantageous to all things being set in place.

Contact with Zachary was finally made and Luther revealed to him that he was Veracity and that there was a greater plan set in place, but the people of Earth needed to be patient. Convincing him took some time but convinced him he did. Luther revealed

previous actions and only because he saw it as beneficial to be on the inside had he not taken a stronger stance.

He also made Zachary understand that he would not just be cast as an outsider but would probably have ended up dead and nothing would have been gained by that. So, this is how he thought a better way of atoning for his errant ways would best be used.

The conversation was only kept amongst Zachary, Cornelius and himself to reduce the risk of exposure. This is where some of the scrolls lack confirmation and Luther's word is all we must go on in many cases.

Pope Zachary & Cornelius

Whether for strategic protection or because of their bond, Zachary and Cornelius were always found standing side by side. Cornelius was quiet but ever vigilant of their surroundings, while Zachary was boisterous and loud, speaking with a sarcastic tone. Everyone was certain that beneath his iron mask, a smile would accompany his words—at least, that was his demeanor before the day the earth grew dark.

Though Zachary had taken up the sobriquet of Pope, it suited him well. Even when Peter was still around, Zachary had been a natural leader. Though he wouldn't speak of it, he too felt that inner calling drawing him to the cause. Of Turkish descent, he had gravitated toward the Vatican after it received its new designation: Fort Vatican. He saw every reason to fight for Old Earth's historical legacy, partly due to his rebellious nature, but mostly because he believed in it. Above all, something in his being didn't trust the Fortunates. When the actual Pope was assassinated on the day the legions stormed the holy city, Zachary knew he needed to be part of what was to come.

On the Day of Decimation, Zachary was among those at the core of the explosion, and he still maintains that he cannot believe he survived. Even with the explanation of DNA mutation, the blast alone should have killed him. Though every inch of his body suffered from that explosion, Zachary picked himself up and walked away.

It was afterward that he met Cornelius. Neither man was aware of their powers initially, and they would discover them in unconventional ways. Cornelius described his first experience as just a wish when he saw a falling stone heading toward a man and knew there was nothing, he could do but hope for more time. The scene then unfolded again, and this time he was able to warn the man—Zachary—of the impending danger. This raises questions about whether these gifts were mere accidents or if the universe had purposefully enabled certain beings to correct what could go wrong.

Together they would eventually stand within Fort Vatican, the fate of the future in their hands. Though none had known what lay beneath the grounds of the walled city, we now know that without Cornelius, the man known as Pope Zachary would never have been able to provide refuge to so many.

He waited for Darrd to contact him again, knowing the next step would require coordination between himself and the Bacchians. Luther had wondered how the Bacchians had managed to enter Goliath undetected and if they could repeat the feat. They explained to him that their transport was a living organism, and being biological, it didn't trigger surveillance mechanisms. Armed with this information, he informed Darrd about the mines outside Ecopolis. Without questioning the science behind it, he trusted their confidence that they could succeed again if attention was diverted.

They began their flight toward Mars, and with precision, Luther caused a malfunction in Apollo. The issue wasn't severe or obvious, but enough to capture the Fortunates' attention. When the Bacchians were within range to enter, he implemented his diversion. A slight sensor triggered in Apollo's foot—the furthest extremity point. As expected, they wouldn't let him investigate alone, so he and Kane ventured to the location. The Fortunates maintained constant contact, all eyes fixed on Apollo—exactly as planned.

Though Mars' atmospheric surveillance detected something, it raised no alarms. The Bacchians traveled once again within their transport, Del Bu Roc—a living being with an inner chamber for the Acolytes. It required no pilot, and its mechanical weaponry remained contained within its outer skin, rendering it undetectable by conventional radar. The surveillance equipment wasn't designed for such detection. While the sudden atmospheric glitch was noted, Apollo's malfunction commanded more attention. The entry succeeded; another potential obstacle overcome.

Due to its size, Del Bu Roc couldn't enter the mines and had to wait on the asteroid Vesta within the asteroid belt. The Fortunates remained oblivious, and the minor diversion served its purpose. Luther's strategic background as a military general had proved invaluable to the operation's smooth execution.

He contacted Zachary to report the Bacchians' successful settlement on Mars. Though appreciative, Zachary feared an imminent attack from the

Fortunates and hoped the next phase would account for this. Luther acknowledged the Fortunates' aggressive nature but reminded him that allowing your enemy to come to you isn't always disadvantageous in warfare—especially while strengthening your defenses, which Zachary certainly was.

While everything progressed according to plan, Luther eagerly anticipated meeting his new allies, but for that, he would need to return to Mars.

THE ORIGIN OF PURITY

With the thought of Goliath being temporarily shut down and war looming on the horizon, Luther decided to return to Mars and share his strategic knowledge. Though the seed had been planted by Luther through Magnus, who had insisted to his brother that if the Fortunates didn't truly trust Luther, what better way to keep watch than having him close to Magnus.

The request for Luther's return to Mars was approved. During his journey back, Darrd reached out while Luther traveled in an Arrow Fighter, accompanied by two Battalion soldiers on either wing as escorts.

Darrd wished to meet and explain the Fortunates' history, just as Luther had hoped. He believed this knowledge would aid their fight against the Fortunates and that Earth's beings should eventually understand it too.

Luther returned to Mars to find heavy activity underway. Meetings among the hierarchy and Endicots were constant. Strategic maneuvers, both offensive and defensive, were being discussed, and arms production had increased. Luther knew he needed to escalate their actions too. Though unaware of exact developments on Earth, he was certain similar preparations were underway.

The bustling affairs provided Luther more opportunities to reach Ecopolis's outer borders unnoticed. Magnus remained his biggest obstacle, being uninvolved in most meetings. Though displeased with their decision, he claimed it was for the better. With Veracity looming and information possibly leaking, they insisted Ecopolis must avoid the disturbances plaguing Terra. This struck a nerve with Magnus, who still felt denied the chance to prove he could suppress all rebellions in his territory. He used the Battalion and the forgotten 13th Legion extensively to maintain order. Luther expressed to Magnus that he should allow him to secure the mines and ensure they were impervious to any external forces and structurally sound, so Ecopolis could withstand an attack. This was a logical precaution that many had not considered as a potential weakness. Surely, Magnus thought, this was why he kept Luther around—his knowledge of battle surpassed that of anyone else, and any past missteps were mere accidents. Still, being cautious by nature, Magnus suggested that the 13th Legion accompany him.

Luther, however, quickly dismissed the suggestion, arguing that the 13th Legion was better suited to patrol the streets of Ecopolis. He proposed taking Battalion soldiers with him instead. It was a reasonable compromise—Battalion soldiers were in surplus, and the people of Ecopolis still held the 13th Legion in high regard.

When Luther reached the border of Ecopolis, preparing to leave the enclosed city, he disarmed the two soldiers accompanying him. Time was of the essence—he needed to reach the Acolytes. While it might not have been necessary, the soldier in him believed that meeting one's allies face-to-face was always wise in war. If Darrd's story could not be told in full, he could always use his gift and communicate with him telepathically.

Upon entering the tunnel, Luther heard a familiar voice—Darrd guiding him through the cavernous passages. A light suddenly illuminated the tunnels, and before him stood Darrd and the Acolytes. They were unlike anything he had imagined. Only one bore the appearance of a man, while the others resembled strange creatures. Yet Luther sensed they posed no threat. Their appearance was irrelevant—what mattered was that they were allies, united by a common enemy.

The first to approach Luther resembled the Fortunates in appearance. His head gleamed like chrome, but from the neck down, he looked more human than the Fortunates ever did. Unlike them, his body was not encased in microorganisms or pulsing with transparency—he was entirely human.

The same could not be said of the others. They were far less human-like.

Darrd extended his hand in greeting, a gesture familiar as a handshake—a welcome contrast to the Fortunates, who had never once offered such a gesture to anyone from Earth. The familiarity stirred something in Luther; he had missed this simple connection, though he had grown accustomed to its absence.

Despite never meeting Darrd before, Luther instinctively knew it was him— he was the first to approach and the only one whose name Luther knew. Darrd proceeded to introduce the others: Deter' Ra La, with reptilian features; Montica Go, insect-like, with multiple limbs; Felle Ha, with a hard-shelled exterior; Bar Bar Tulu, a being seemingly from the deepest parts of the ocean; and Guluada, a massive four-legged creature. These were his allies, and now Luther wanted to hear their story.

Darrd began recounting the ancient history of their conflict. The Fortunates were the original inhabitants of Mars, having lived there for over three and a half cosmic revolutions. At that time, only Mars and Terra—now known as Earth— harbored life in the solar system. But a disaster loomed. A small planet between Mars and Jupiter, called Discordia, was weakening. Each time Jupiter and Mars aligned, Discordia's fragile atmosphere tore further apart. The Martians feared that the next alignment would destroy the planet entirely, sending dangerous debris toward Mars.

Faced with this impending catastrophe, the Martians debated their options. They could either evacuate Mars entirely or settle on Terra. They had always regarded Terra as inferior—its inhabitants were animalistic, lacking the cognitive ability to develop into intelligent beings. However, Terra's environment shared enough similarities with Mars to make it a viable new home.

Rather than migrating immediately, the Martians devised a plan: they would use the creatures of Terra as incubators for their embryos, testing whether Martian life could survive in Terra's atmosphere. This process would also allow the Martians to build immunity to Terra's environment before making it their permanent home. Over time, these incubated beings could serve as laborers, constructing structures and preparing the land for the Martians' arrival.

Everything proceeded according to the plan of King Patience and his chief advisor, Fortitude. But dissent arose among the people of Mars. They feared that the embryos, having developed inside Terran creatures, would carry impure, mixed blood. Rumors spread that Martian scientists were not merely planting embryos but engaging in forbidden relations with the Terran hosts. Though unproven, these rumors fueled a movement against settling on Terra.

Eventually, the Martians abandoned their plan to colonize Terra. Instead, they chose to leave the solar system entirely, vowing to return one day, reclaim their lost home, and purge the universe of any impurities. They left behind a small group of scientists stationed on Terra, in regions later known as the Mediterranean and Mesopotamia—the cradles of civilization. Over time, these scientists' descendants would give rise to the Sumerians, Phoenicians, Egyptians, Greeks, and Romans, though there were many turns before the current.

The Martians embarked on their exodus in a massive vessel called the Ark, accompanied by smaller ships. They brought with them every comfort from Mars, including pairs of animals to populate their new world. Their philosophy—that all life forms were interconnected—guided them through their journey and would shape their future home.

As Luther listened to Darrd's account, he realized that the Martians' story bore striking similarities to Earth's biblical narratives. It was as if the ancient tales of Mars had been passed down through generations, becoming Earth's own history over time. Luther began to see the story of humanity from a new perspective.

Though Darrd and the Bacchians could not help Luther fully understand his planet's history, some things were becoming clearer. It now made sense why the Fortunates were so evasive when questioned about Earth's past— it was their own history. The Martians had seeded life on Earth, and they believed it was their duty to cleanse the universe of any impurity they had created.

Darrd admitted that the complete history of the Martians' journey and struggles was lost to time, but he knew that the exiled Martians eventually settled on a new planet called Fortuna. It was there that Darrd's own story—

and the conflict with their neighboring planet, Bacchus—began.

Bacchus appeared desolate, plagued by volcanic eruptions, with its strange inhabitants initially dismissed as mindless creatures. However, the Bacchians' society existed beneath the planet's surface, hidden from view. Though different from the Martians' civilization, it was a society nonetheless.

Luther knew it was time to return to Ecopolis and reactivate the Battalion soldiers he had disarmed. The insights he had gained about the Fortunates were invaluable, but there was more to learn—particularly about how the Fortunates' sense of superiority had influenced their actions.

Now that he had met Darrd and the Acolytes in person, future communications could safely take place telepathically. Darrd continued to share what he knew, offering a concise but vital history. Luther planned to relay some of this knowledge to Zachary in due time, but he needed to understand the full picture before acting on it.

It was crucial for Luther to gather information about the Fortunates' current status and plans, ensuring Earth could trust and collaborate with them. He would consult Magnus regularly for further insights, though Magnus remained fixated on using Zeus to destroy Earth. Magnus's frustration with the Fortunates was evident—he seemed to know more about Zeus than he let on, a fact that would only become clear later in the war.

For now, the Battalion soldiers maintained control over the streets of Ecopolis, with the approval of the Fortunates. Those stationed in Tropaion were carefully vetted, while those in Ecopolis lived among Earth's inhabitants as second-class citizens. They would be granted refuge only when the war began in earnest.

Darrd confided to Luther that he had become a Bacchian by circumstance. As one of the Fortunates' chief scientists, he had once served under Alpha, the former king of Fortuna and father of the current ruler, Icon. It was during Alpha's reign that Darrd had pioneered the science responsible for the Fortunates' transformation, and his own.

Being fully biological yet resembling robots due to the chrome-encased brains all Fortunates possessed was the foundation of their micro-biotic system. This scientific advancement involved microscopic cells designed to attach or detach upon damage, either repairing or replacing the damaged tissue. As a result, some Fortunates appeared more robotic than human. Darrd was held in the highest regard among the Fortunates, as the people of Fortuna became nearly immortal. The micro-biotics were housed within their still-organic brains, encased in metal to ensure continuous cellular regeneration. This marvel extended down the spine, ensuring that all extremities were sustained via the central nervous system.

Though disease no longer posed a threat, they were not truly immortal. If the head were severed along with the vertebrae, the body would collapse like any other biological being. However, such an outcome was unlikely outside of battle.

After Darrd's creation of this new science and his rise to prominence, he was tasked with pursuing a new breakthrough that would elevate the Fortunates to elite status among galactic species. It was then proposed that they attack Bacchus, their neighboring planet, and eliminate what they saw as an inferior species. However, Darrd's moral compass found no value in destroying the Bacchians merely because they were deemed lesser. The Bacchians had never posed a threat to Fortuna since settling in the same solar system. To Darrd, the suggestion to attack them reflected the same misguided intentions the Fortunates harbored toward Terra thousands of years ago.

The Fortunates constantly reminded their citizens of history, especially when dealing with Earthlings. Yet, they omitted the truth—that they viewed Earthlings as inferior beings and believed it was their mission to cleanse the universe. It was not just a fleeting idea to eliminate others who shared their star system but a calling they pursued with unwavering dedication.

Before proceeding to exterminate the Bacchians, the Fortunates discovered that the Bacchians possessed abilities they lacked—particularly the gift of mind-to-mind communication, a power mastered by the man we would come to know and the messenger of the Fortunates, Adom. Ironically, the Bacchians might have shared this ability if the Fortunates had simply asked.

Despite their formidable appearance, the Bacchians were largely peaceful. Even though the Fortunates were outsiders in the solar system, the Bacchians saw no reason to interfere and instead focused on their own lives. But that was not the way of the Fortunates—especially the High Fortunates.

Unfortunately, Darrd lacked the authority to reject their demands, though he occasionally voiced his opposition. The Fortunates launched several expeditions to Bacchus with the aim of capturing Bacchians for study. These missions often resulted in the deaths of the subjects, as the experiments required extracting their brains. The same apparatus used in these procedures that had once been employed on Warlord's brain—an operation known as the Electronic Stimulation Process (E.S.P.). This technology allowed surgeons to extract individual cells to control their host's actions or, in the Warlord's case, enhance abilities through electronic impulses.

It was later believed that similar experiments had been performed on Earthlings for different purposes. During abductions of government officials and influential individuals, the Fortunates extracted memory cells, gaining access to memories the subjects were unaware they possessed. That is what had occurred during the time that Panspermia lay seemingly dormant during its initial entry to the solar system of Copernicus. Those days that it settled near the outer planets were by design before progressing to Mars and eventually to the day of Adom's contact. Through these cells, the Fortunates unlocked historical knowledge—spanning from the arrival of the Martians on Terra to their eventual departure. While prominent abductees were returned after testing, nameless individuals were discarded, vanishing without a trace.

When Darrd vehemently opposed these studies back on Fortuna, he fell out of favor with the Fortunates. Unbothered by his loss of status, he escalated his protest. Despite knowing the risks—severe punishment or even execution—he refused to stand by as atrocities were committed. His defiance culminated in a decisive act: Darrd beheaded Alpha, the leader of the Fortunates.

The death of their long-reigning ruler threw Fortuna into chaos. Alpha's son, Icon, was the sole heir, and the transition of power occurred almost overnight. Icon ascended to the throne and immediately sought to eliminate Darrd. His execution was planned as a public spectacle, a ceremony meant to both punish and humiliate Darrd.

Darrd's only regret was that he had acted impulsively, leaving no opportunity to explain his motives to others. His execution would likely be framed as the result of madness, with none knowing the truth behind his actions. However, it was Agatha, Icon's wife and now Queen of Fortuna, who proposed an alternative punishment. Her suggestion would become both her undoing and the downfall of Fortuna itself.

Agatha decreed that Darrd be exiled to Bacchus, condemned to live among the very beings he sought to save. His punishment was intended to prolong his suffering, forcing him to live in fear, never knowing when or how his end would come. A ceremonial procession marked his departure as he walked through the streets of Tropaion toward the vessel that would transport him to his doom. Crowds jeered at him along the way, mocking him with the technology he had created. Though Darrd's head still bore the same chrome encasing as the other

Fortunates, his ability to regenerate cells had been reduced to a minimal state, causing his skin to appear more natural than theirs.

The Fortunates hoped that Darrd would fall prey to the Randars—a species known for their slow digestive process, which left their prey alive for much of the ordeal. Randars resembled snakes with legs, their elongated torsos functioning as digestive tracts. Though not aggressive, they swept the barren Bacchian terrain for sustenance, occasionally consuming living creatures by accident.

Upon being dropped onto Bacchus, Darrd searched for shelter, believing it was only a matter of time before he met his end—either at the hands of a Bacchian species or through starvation. He assumed that, given the Fortunates' hostility, the Bacchians would see him as a threat and kill him on sight.

Then, just as Luther had once heard a voice call to him at Goliath's gate, Darrd experienced something similar. A voice reached out to him telepathically. It was the Acolyte Felle Ha, and her message was simple yet profound:

Fortunate, Fortunate, Fortunate. We know why you are here.

In that moment, Darrd felt a strange sense of comfort, realizing that his fate might not be sealed after all. Keeping him alive, he believed, would ultimately lead to the downfall of the Fortunates.

In the days that followed, Darrd adapted to life among the Bacchians. Meanwhile, Icon assumed Darrd had perished and was dismayed that he could not witness the death of the man who had killed his father. Icon continued conducting experiments and launching occasional raids on Bacchus. However, the Bacchians' subterranean dwellings, shielded by the planet's rocky surface, provided them with protection from such attacks—protection they had maintained for centuries.

The Fortunates only landed on Bacchus to abduct specimens for study, though these missions grew less frequent over time. With their mastery of electronic pulses, the Fortunates no longer needed physical subjects to stimulate another's mind—the very skill the Bacchians had used as a natural form of communication from birth was now a learned skill of the Fortunates.

Darrd remained hidden below the surface to avoid jeopardizing any invasion efforts, knowing that revealing he was still alive could undermine their strategy. It was there that the Bacchians taught him this method of communication, and it was also there that he began contemplating ways to combat the Fortunates. He realized they would not stop until their labeled enemies ceased to exist. This was crucial information for the people of Earth—understanding that the Fortunates' relentless pursuit of dominance was their way of life. It was this realization that prompted Darrd to tell Luther:

I have seen it before. The monsters that you hate are the ones they create.

Luther repeated those words in his mind, over and over, knowing they revealed the harsh truth: the Fortunates needed to be eliminated. It wasn't just their existence that was dangerous, but their way of thinking. That ideology had to be extinguished, not the other way around. Perspective is everything—it shapes how one views right and wrong. Perhaps there were no absolutes, only perception.

Darrd explained that a shift in time between the two worlds was imminent, all because of a fatal decision Agatha had made by extending his life for their own malicious intent. She and they wanted Darrd to not just be exterminated, but to suffer.

Deep beneath Bacchus, Darrd collaborated with the Bacchians. His first task was to convince them that neutrality would only lead to their extinction. The Fortunates would continue their onslaught until no Bacchians remained. Darrd tried to make them understand that, unlike the Bacchians—who sought only to live peacefully—the Fortunates believed they were purifying the universe. In their eyes, only the superior deserved to exist, and they alone determined what was superior, judging not only intelligence but appearance.

This purging wasn't just ideological; it was practical. Inferior beings, the Fortunates claimed, hindered the universe's progress. Their eradication was necessary to build a utopia for those who remained.

Many Bacchians resisted Darrd's warnings, insisting they had survived this long without engaging in war and that starting one would bring only death. But Darrd warned them: the Fortunates' science was advancing, and they planned every day for the Bacchians' extinction.

While some Bacchians eventually came around to Darrd's view, they faced another obstacle—they lacked the capacity for warfare. The Bacchians had no weapons, nor had they ever seen the need for them. Peace had defined their existence. This was where Darrd saw an opportunity.

He studied their biology and discovered their cells could regenerate rapidly—a feature that inspired his advancements in micro-biotics and immunity. Darrd used this knowledge to his advantage, experimenting with ways to weaponize the Bacchians. He developed biological weapons that could remain hidden beneath their skin, extending from their limbs or bodies when needed and then retracting. Although Bacchians had many subspecies, their DNA was remarkably similar, with only minor mutations based on where their tribes lived on Bacchus.

Darrd's most ambitious creation involved transforming larger Bacchians into living vehicles for their smaller kin, much like what he achieved with Del Bu Roc, though Luther had not yet encountered this marvel. These adaptations ensured that even the most peaceful Bacchians were now ready to defend themselves at any moment.

This change tipped the balance. When the Fortunates returned to Bacchus for what they thought would be another easy raid—this time to harvest Begot eggs, a delicacy on Fortuna—they were met with a shock. The Begots, a typically docile subspecies, revealed their hidden weapons. What had once been a routine expedition turned into a disaster for the Fortunates. Two of their number were killed, and the rest fled, marking the end of Bacchus as prey.

With that, the war between the two worlds began. When the Bacchians emerged from their underground shelters, armed and prepared, the Fortunates realized their mission of universal cleansing would be far more difficult than anticipated.

Darrd advised the Bacchians to not accept any truce the Fortunates might offer. Knowing the Fortunates' mentality, it would only be temporary, and for their gain to better position themselves. Emboldened by their newfound strength, and the words of Darrd, they chose to go on the offensive.

Despite their surprise, the Fortunates still had the upper hand. They possessed greater numbers and advanced technology. But if the Bacchians ever reached the surface of Fortuna, it could spell the Fortunates' doom. For now, the Bacchians relied on creatures like Del Bu Roc for transportation, and while they were many, they were still living beings— war was not in their nature. Darrd could not, in good conscience, force them to fight if they were unwilling.

During this time, rumors began to circulate among the Fortunates about the survival of their kind, invoking the names of Patience and Fortitude, ancient leaders who had once led them from to their home on Mars. Now, the Fortunates looked to Mars once more.

Darrd didn't know exactly what had driven the Fortunates to this decision, as his information came only from surveillance, not direct observation. The full story remained on Fortuna or within the Golden Tower, hidden from view.

When Panspermia—their massive starship—was built, some believed it marked the Fortunates' exodus. But Darrd suspected otherwise. If they were truly abandoning Fortuna, they would have built hundreds of such ships. Instead, Darrd saw Panspermia as part of a larger plan and made it his mission to uncover their true intentions.

The Bacchians agreed not to pursue the Fortunates if they left, though Darrd doubted they would ever truly leave anything unfinished. The Fortunates were methodical and patient, willing to wait decades or even centuries to achieve their goals.

Through the Bacchians' ability to read electrical thought patterns, they discovered that the Fortunates were returning to Mars, and then use a device called David and Goliath to bend space. However, they lacked precise coordinates for Mars, prompting them to embark on a quest that eventually led them to Luther's solar system—known to them as Copernicus, the home of Terra.

Darrd knew the Fortunates' intentions could not be good, and the war was far from over. Even though one ship had left, many more would follow, carrying with them the ambition to dominate once the bridge was complete. Adom and others volunteered for the quest, knowing it would take decades. But the Fortunates' patience ensured they would persist, seeking not only allies but also resources that could be found only in their origin solar system.

The Fortunates believed their destiny lay in acquiring something essential from these worlds—perhaps even completing a quantum weapon that required a unique energy found only here. This, too, remained a mystery, one better left unsolved.

The war between Bacchus and Fortuna raged on, shaping a new generation of Bacchians who knew only conflict. The Fortunates, accustomed to a life of conquest, taught their young that purging the universe was their duty. For the Bacchians, however, this life was unfamiliar—they fought not out of belief, but because survival demanded it.

Over the next ten Earth years, as Bacchus and Fortuna aligned more closely in orbit, battles escalated. Each side launched attacks, retreated, and regrouped, resulting in eight major wars since the Fortunates' initial invasion, with another added after crossing through Goliath.

Luther now understood why the Fortunates seemed relieved when they crossed Goliath's threshold. They were

fleeing from a war, believing they had found refuge.

Armed with this knowledge, Luther knew his next step: to share the truth with the world.

TRUTH TO BE TOLD

Luther methodically developed a chronological schedule for releasing information, carefully considering whom to inform first. Strategic planning was crucial—revealing details to the wrong people prematurely could trigger reactions far beyond what they were prepared to handle.

He determined the safest course would be to reach out to Zachary first, ensuring the earthlings understood the futility of negotiating with the Fortunates. The Day of Decimation had proven their genocidal intentions, and their failed attempt wouldn't deter them from completing their mission. Luther now understood that the extinction of a race wasn't merely their goal, it was their very purpose.

This could be corroborated by Jacob's scrolls, now preserved in the Vatican, rather than relying solely on Luther's word. Once informed of the Fortunates' history and Mars's ancient past, Zachary would bear the responsibility of informing humanity. He chose to deliver a cautionary speech, though less detailed than Luther's account. These details were recorded in the scrolls but released much later, with careful notation that the information came from Luther rather than firsthand experience— unlike most previous scroll entries. When information came from outside sources, as with Jacob's accounts, the origin was always clearly attributed to more trusted sources than Luther. Zachary's trust in Luther remained tenuous, given his history as Magnus's brother and his role in orchestrating attacks against his own people.

Later records would reveal that Zachary regularly documented information in the scrolls at its discovery, though he controlled the timing of its release to the public.

Luther remained indifferent to how Zachary utilized the information, only concerning himself with earthly matters when coordinating attacks. He recognized his precarious position, knowing neither side fully trusted him despite his conviction that he now served the right cause. Should the war end with a clear victor, he faced potential punishment from either side if his role was exposed.

His next objective was to gather intelligence about the Fortunates through his brother, though this required extreme caution. Magnus's loyalty remained questionable, and the Fortunates harbored suspicions about both Carter brothers. Luther knew Magnus would readily betray him to regain the Fortunates' trust. This necessitated careful questioning and even more prudent use of any information obtained.

Magnus's aggressive, unrestrained nature occasionally led to careless revelations. One such instance occurred when he mentioned Zeus's potential use against Earth, questioning the Fortunates' reluctance to deploy it. When Luther suggested this might reflect Zeus's limited capabilities, Magnus impetuously revealed the weapon's true nature. The revelation stunned Luther—Zeus far exceeded its supposed nuclear capabilities. Magnus explained that the weapon employed quantum physics, utilizing dark matter to engulf planets upon impact. The result would either cause complete planetary implosion within the space-time continuum or, at minimum, reduce all life forms to cellular fragments that would dissipate like ash.

<u>ACOLYTES</u>

Luther Carter made history as the first person to interact with a Bacchian, initially through voice alone. This proved fortunate, as Bacchians could be intimidating in appearance, even Darrd, the former Fortunate among them. The group's choice of name—Acolytes—reflected their inclusive philosophy, refusing to identify with any single world and instead embracing the universe as a whole.

Darrd explained his careful selection of Luther as a contact. Rather than reading Luther's mind, he had studied his speech patterns while between the portal rings. Though Bacchians rejected the Fortunates' belief in superiority and their mission to cleanse the universe of impurity, Darrd's time on Bacchus had given him unique insights. He spoke of cosmic symmetry—not predestined fate, but rather the universe's tendency to present choices at crucial moments. While some might attribute this to individual character, Darrd believed the soul remained connected to this universal energy. Through this understanding, he had sensed Luther's trustworthiness before their actual meeting.

Darrd's importance to both the Bacchians and the universe cannot be overstated. His banishment to Bacchus proved crucial to this historical narrative, laying another steppingstone toward humanity's inevitable universal journey. The fateful decision by Icon and Agatha, celebrated by the Fortunate population, had initially seemed Darrd's downfall. However, his choice to assassinate Alpha, though regrettable, ultimately paved the way for saving planets across multiple solar systems.

His brilliant mind found purpose among the Bacchians, who needed more than just protection from hostile neighbors. Darrd befriended these supposedly barbaric monsters, as the Fortunates viewed them, discovering them to be both peaceful and highly intelligent. They simply prioritized practical survival over intellectual pursuits. Recognizing the Fortunates' genocidal intentions, Darrd convinced many Bacchians to adapt their thinking to ensure their survival. None embraced this evolution more thoroughly than the seven who would journey with him through the portal as the Acolytes.

Bacchus hosted numerous species beneath its surface, most living in respectful coexistence. The Randars were the exception, keeping to their own tunnels and surviving primarily on surface vegetation—though they wouldn't reject other prey that crossed their path. Unlike other species, they lacked electronic brainwave communication abilities and were entirely non-verbal. This made Bacchus appear uninhabited from above, despite its thriving underground civilization.

The six species accompanying Darrd as Acolytes represented diverse regions of the underground world. Drawing comparisons to Leviathan's current inhabitants, each species possessed unique characteristics:

Montica Go resembled an ant-like insect, distinguished by two additional limbs extending from its back. Its head could rotate a full 360 degrees, and its back limbs, longer than the others—could transform from weapons to legs, allowing it to shift from bipedal to quadrupedal movement while maintaining defensive capabilities.

Bar Bar TuLu appeared as though it had emerged from Earth's oceans onto land, making its home in the depths of Delara near a steaming water stream.

Telea Ha, one of the winged Bacchians, dwelled closest to the surface. They occasionally ventured above ground to gather piatals—leaf-like structures that grew directly from Bacchus's ash-covered surface, essential for maintaining the underground atmosphere. Their insect-like frame, similar to a mantis, would have seemed somewhat familiar to earthlings, though unlike Montica Go, they possessed no additional limbs.

Gulu Ada, perhaps the most striking, had no fixed home but patrolled the underworld. Its golden coat emanated a self-illuminating glow. The creature's unique anatomy featured a torso with arms protruding above a horse-like lower body, complete with hooves and powerful legs. Its face contained multiple eyes, creating an extraordinary appearance. During the invasion of Tropaion, Darrd rode Gulu Ada through the city streets, together defeating fleeing Fortunates.

Felle Ha, another occassional surface-dwelling species, possessed a distinctive shell and large jaws that formed a sack-like neck where it housed its eggs.

The final two species capable of flight were Deter' RaLa and Del Bu Roc. They primarily flew within the underworld's vast central cone that extended down to Delara's core stream. While Deter' RaLa, a sleek creature combining features of both elephant and reptile, flew regularly, Del Bu Roc—the largest of all species—flew less frequently. Not all Del Bu Roc possessed flight capability, and they showed remarkable variation in appearance while maintaining their massive size.

The underground realm, possibly called Delara, was structured around this central cone, with stairways connecting various levels and tunnels leading to species-specific dwelling areas. Each section opened into its own governed world. The separation of species wasn't based on superiority but on biological compatibility for breeding purposes. Del Bu Roc proved particularly fascinating in this regard, as their diverse appearances didn't prevent successful internal breeding, often producing offspring with novel characteristics.

The Bacchians' biology differed significantly from known life forms, featuring unique cellular structures and various reproductive methods, including some species' ability to self-fertilize eggs asexually, as demonstrated by Felle Ha's species.

Some uncertainty remains about whether Delara referred to the underground world or the planet itself, which the Fortunates later named Bacchus—a more fitting name given its connection to the god of agriculture and wine, and its closer alignment with Fortunate linguistics than Bacchian language.

These beings became Earth's new allies. Despite their unfamiliarity with each world, they encountered, matching Earth's own uncertainty, they all united under the identity of Leviathanians, transcending their visible differences.

Luther recognized the critical importance of warning Earth about Zeus's capabilities. Despite the Fortunates' reluctance to deploy it, the weapon's mere existence demanded preparation for potential planetary evacuation. Upon contacting Zachary, Luther detailed Zeus's devastating power while cautioning against attempts to merely disable it. The quantum physics involved remained largely mysterious, and interfering with such forces could have unpredictable consequences for Earth or even the universe itself—perhaps explaining the Fortunates' hesitation to use it.

Surprisingly, Zachary's reaction seemed oddly measured, showing no increased fear despite learning of this devastating threat. This struck Luther as peculiar, suggesting that the Pope and Cornelius had preparations in place beyond anyone's knowledge—information they kept not only from Luther but from Earth's population as well.

Luther began to understand the Fortunates' reluctance to fully deploy Zeus, connecting it to what Darrd had revealed about the war beyond the portal. Their situation there appeared even more dire than the conflict in this solar system, as Agatha had inadvertently hinted to Magnus earlier.

This realization led Luther to believe Darrd needed to be informed, and that a coordinated strike against the Goliath portal might be necessary to protect Bacchus. Darrd confirmed knowledge of such weapons being developed by

Fortunate scientists, though they were in early stages before his banishment. He explained that quantum entanglement restrictions had initially hindered development, suggesting this might have motivated their original journey to this solar system. The danger of a quantum bomb, Darrd warned, extended beyond mere destruction—it could create universal devastation through scattered black holes and space-time distortions.

The risk of sending Zeus through the portal remained unknown. The interaction between the quantum weapon and the portal's energy field could potentially trigger universal implosion or, at minimum, destroy both connected solar systems. Despite these uncertainties, Darrd emphasized the necessity of destroying Goliath— an objective Earth needed to consider if they hadn't already.

As a skilled general, Luther knew the importance of adapting strategy when presented with new information. He immediately reconnected with Zachary, making this their primary objective, while remaining vigilant about potential Fortunate countermoves.

While developing the assault plan for Goliath, Luther revived Veracity to keep the Fortunates defensive and confused. This psychological warfare tactic forced them to consider multiple scenarios rather than executing a single plan, potentially creating opportunities through their uncertainty.

The reborn Veracity began exposing the Fortunates' past, particularly challenging their sanitized version of the Day of Decimation told to Mars's people. While Martians weren't openly rebellious toward the Fortunates, this stemmed largely from carefully manipulated information suggesting Earth's combative nature had led to self-destruction.

As Luther continued releasing information, more Veracity followers emerged, donning masks and sharing their own knowledge. The Fortunates pressured Magnus to regain control, warning him against allowing another Vatican situation—a threat whose exact nature remained unclear.

In response to growing unrest in Ecopolis, Magnus began labeling Terra-born Martians as "half-breeds," despite potentially falling into this category himself. This pleased the

High Fortunates but strained relations with the 13th Legion. When this proved insufficient, he authorized Battalion Soldiers to patrol streets and arrest suspected threats, reducing the Legion to purely pursuing Veracity.

The Fortunates observed these developments from Tropaion, protected by Endicots Lair but increasingly convinced that only pure Martian blood could be trusted. This mirrored historical pattern of empire collapse through overextension and internal division, echoing Earth's Roman Empire—though such lessons often go unheeded, leading to repeated bloodshed.

Importantly, while no violent protests occurred, people simply sought truth, identifying with Peter's fundamental question: "Why?" The Fortunates continued portraying Earth's rebels as primitive, particularly mocking Zachary's throne. However, this "Throne Mountain," crafted from Zagros Mountains rock by Jacob, stood majestically in Fort Vatican's Snake Room—its cratered exterior contrasting with smooth marble seating that gleamed under light.

The contrast between venues proved striking: Fort Vatican's austere grandeur versus the Golden Tower's court, where six seats backed by a rising sun motif demonstrated Fortunate opulence. Luther recalled his own trial's magnificence as Ajax, Adom, Icon, Agatha, Peripheral, and Echo determined his fate, though this diminished neither the Snake Room's nor Throne Mountain's impact, where Zachary still sat with Cornelius at his side.

These events would soon transform the cold war into planetary bloodshed as truth continued to emerge.

A CALL TO ARMS

Pope Zachary Damir addressed Earth's population with a message balancing hope and reality. Though no formal committee existed, his leadership style wasn't autocratic—he served as the people's voice, always considering opposition when planning their path forward. Such opposition rarely materialized, as the population recognized his dedication to their interests, with Cornelius tempering any emotional decisions. Zachary's position stemmed from his good standing with Peter before the Day of Decimation and his subsequent close relationship with Jacob. Rather than formal anointment, his papal title emerged naturally, supported by his newfound ability to control earth's elements. He assumed the religious throne at a time when traditional religion had diminished in importance.

In his address, Damir emphasized the Fortunates' unwavering commitment to Earth's destruction, rejecting any possibility of peaceful coexistence between separate kingdoms. His rousing speech rallied the Earthlings for an offensive strategy to end the conflict decisively. While sharing Luther's historical discoveries, he carefully omitted both the source and any mention of the Bacchians' presence.

His assembly concluded with the recorded declaration:
If it's genocide the Fortunates want, then genocide they will receive.

Despite the world's unified support behind these words, Zachary understood the near impossibility of defeating the Fortunates. He assembled experts in strategic warfare, physics, and science necessary for launching planetary attacks. They tested how their powers might function in space or alternate atmospheres, drawing lessons from the Apostles' lunar strike, which had revealed limitations in their abilities.

Meanwhile, the Fortunates prepared for full-scale warfare, recognizing they faced more than a simple attack on Terra. They needed comprehensive defenses against a newly weaponized planet.

They accelerated Battalion Soldier production and fighter manufacturing, deploying forces to both Zeus and the previously underutilized Panspermia, which orbited Mars like an additional moon. The latter's activation acknowledged Earth's capacity for interplanetary travel via Tiburon. Uncertainty about Terra's capabilities plagued them—could the Pope be constructing hidden facilities below ground? Were the current Apostles truly the strongest mutants on Earth? They positioned Zeus to maintain constant surveillance over Earth's Mediterranean region, anticipating potential strike trajectories.

While developing defensive strategies, they recognized Earth's aggressive posturing required proactive measures.

However, their approach remained cautious, acknowledging Zeus as their last remaining Guardian following Ares' and Hades' destruction, with Apollo permanently stationed near Goliath. They understood the Battalion's limitations as mere pawns buying reaction time, especially compared to the Apostles' or other mutants' capabilities.

The G.O.D.S. remained their most effective weapons, as Martian blood couldn't survive in Earth's atmosphere—any attack would rely entirely on technology. Throughout this preparation, Magnus continued advocating for Zeus's deployment despite Agatha's warnings. Even with legitimate concerns about threats beyond Goliath, Earth remained an immediate challenge requiring attention.

Both sides waited, and then it happened. Peripheral visited Apollo to begin what must have been an uncomfortable conversation with Kane. He informed Kane that he would be relieved of his duties manning Apollo and would instead join the first attack on Terra alongside the rest of the G.O.D.S. Their sole objective: infiltrate the Vatican and uncover any secrets lying within or beneath its walls.

Kane must have responded with bewilderment about leading such a charge. Had they discovered a way around the atmospheric oppression that had killed anyone with Martian blood? Had they developed protective technology that would allow his exposure, and if so, why not pursue it with the Endicots? Most importantly, was he simply more expendable?

The air was thick with war on both planets, and only time would reveal when and how events would unfold. Both sides could only wait and wait they did. There were no negotiations, but neither were there aggressive acts. Some foolishly believed this was how things could remain, but a decision had already been made—this was not a time of peace or complacency. War was coming, without question. The scrolls referred to this period as the "State of Ataraxy," but it was also a time of preparation.

Then Peripheral revealed the truth: Kane himself was one of the G.O.D.S.—the pinnacle of their creation. Although it now explained why he didn't wear the chrome head of the Fortunates, Kane was disoriented to learn he wasn't one of them. He had been programmed with memories and what he believed was free thinking, only to discover he was another weaponized soldier created by the Fortunates. This revelation left him perplexed and questioning everything.

The Fortunates saw Kane as more than just an experiment—he was their theoretical ideal made real. Even the people of Fortuna who weren't previously informed of Kane's android nature couldn't recognize it. More significantly, neither could the transplanted Earthlings. This meant the synthetics would allow Fortunates to walk freely among Earthlings. It would cause Earthlings to become unsettled and suspicious of their own kind—a strategy that proved successful, as we now know from our travels that suspicion lies in the heart of almost every Earthling.

Kane returned to Panspermia with nearly all the Arrows that had been guarding Goliath. With Goliath currently non-functional, they believed protecting Mars took priority over guarding the portal. They also assumed Earth's capabilities for coordinating multiple strikes were limited, and that by placing Terra under siege, Apollo would provide adequate defense.

Luther quickly informed Zachary about Goliath's reduced defenses—if they ever had an opportunity to strike, this was it. They knew the portal would soon be resupplied due to the increased production of Arrow Fighters and Battalion soldiers.

Earth was no longer equipped with just shuttles and Tiburon. Warlord had created a fleet of Stealthlord Fighters, capable of cloaking and avoiding enemy detection. However, the cloaking had time limitations, requiring precise timing to outrun the faster Arrows while approaching Goliath.

Meanwhile, the G.O.D.S. assembled within Panspermia, preparing to launch toward Zeus and ultimately Terra. A massive contingent of Battalion Soldiers would accompany them, bringing war back to Earth's ground. After much deliberation about strategy, they decided to concentrate their greatest forces on Earth. The Endicots split their forces between maintaining Endicots Lair and reinforcing Panspermia, where they would man Arrow Fighters as a final defense line against potential space vessel attacks.

The day finally arrived when waiting became a thing of the past, and full-scale war began. Both sides braced for the imminent arrival of death. This prompted Zachary to turn to Cornelius and speak what became some of the most memorable words recorded in the scrolls, as Clone had often documented even without instruction: *History books are written by the victor. Let's hope, Cornelius, that it is our story being told.*

Before Kane's departure, Luther was summoned to review final instructions about gaining tactical advantages. As Earth's greatest field general, Luther was certain that Kane had reminded the others before their final ascension that although they weren't flesh and blood, they were still Fortunates in every way—and possibly the future. Kane undoubtedly repeated these words to himself, the same words spoken by High Fortunates like Icon and Agatha before his departure.

More names worthy of remembrance were about to be lost on the day the G.O.D.S. landed on Earth. Ten shuttles and four Stealthlord fighters launched immediately from Earth. While Battalion soldiers were still boarding vessels to support Kane's group of mercenaries, Zeus couldn't engage.

The Stealthlord fighters activated their cloaking and remained hidden from the surrounding Arrows, but the shuttles weren't so fortunate—some were destroyed almost immediately upon leaving Earth's atmosphere.

They raced straight toward Mars with Arrows in pursuit. Suddenly, the Battalion-manned fighters were caught off guard as the Stealthlord fighters revealed themselves and engaged the Arrows in battle. When word reached Mars of the situation, their previous confidence against a small group of minimally armed shuttles quickly evaporated. A fleet of Arrow fighters, now manned by Endicots, launched from Panspermia to meet the incoming attack.

Meanwhile, the remaining Battalion forces had fully boarded Tundra and landed on Earth's surface to begin their assault. An armed Earthling army awaited them, leaving Kane and his group to clash with the Apostles. Tundra was essentially a massive hollow transport vessel, capable of moving great numbers of passengers. While equipped with defensive firearms, its cannons were nothing like the other war machines built for attack. Tundra's primary function was transport—its cargo was its weapon.

The G.O.D.S. and this group of Apostles had never encountered each other before, and some believed this group was more powerful than its predecessors and more skilled in hand-to-hand combat. However, the Apostles had never faced someone like Kane, who had been held back from the previous battle and possessed superior skills to all others.

Since most Earthlings lacked the extreme abilities of the Apostles, the battle between them and the Battalion soldiers resembled wars of old, resulting in many lost lives. Each group remained isolated in its task, demonstrating both aggressive attacks and skilled defense. Some circles came to call it "The Three Battles to War," though it never achieved the fame of the Battle of Gibraltar—likely because most felt the war had begun long ago.

Magnus began playing a crucial role as events unfolded. Seeing the unrest growing within Ecopolis, he implemented martial law. All inhabitants were ordered to retreat to their homes, and when Veracity still appeared, he escalated these actions to include invasions of every family's home to account for all residents. This decision would later prove pivotal in the confrontation.

The race toward Mars—at least as the Fortunates saw it—became the immediate focus. The Endicots proved less adept at piloting the flying machines than their robotic counterparts. Perhaps this was because, as living beings, they wouldn't act with the same reckless abandonment as machines, or maybe they were simply less familiar with the fighters and slower to react. Either way, this allowed the small convoy to breach the first wave of interceptors, causing unprecedented nervousness among the Fortunates.

Icon ordered Goliath to be prepared for entry—a preemptive move for possible evacuation. Though it never reached that point, this decision transformed what was meant to be a simple drive toward Goliath's destruction into something far more significant than Zachary had planned.

Battles raged on all fronts with no clear victories until one of the G.O.D.S. fell. An Apostle known as Masquerade, whose power allowed her to impersonate anyone she witnessed, took Kane's form to get close to one of the G.O.D.S. Catching them off guard, she used her dagger-like weapons to pierce its outer layer from waist to shoulders, allowing Darter to rip out its lifeline, essentially its spinal cord—leaving the android lifeless with no possibility of regeneration.

This loss prompted Kane to order the retrieval of all others. Though they were meant to fight to the death, perhaps Peripheral had exceeded his own expectations. He had allowed his creation to become too real, and what was meant to be just a machine had developed feelings—including fear. Kane's calculated reaction focused on preserving and protecting his companions.

While the Fortunates were disappointed by this outcome, they faced more pressing issues as their world came under attack. The shuttles pressed forward relentlessly; despite knowing they faced complete opposition as they approached Mars. As they prepared to clash with the severely outnumbering Fortunates, the four Stealthlord Fighters suddenly changed course toward Goliath. Four of the surviving shuttles joined them, while about ten continued forward. The Fortunates realized the true nature of the attack—the shuttles were missiles targeting Panspermia. The divided Arrows hesitated for a crucial moment, failing to destroy the

projectiles. Six struck the terraformed vessel, delivering a devastating blow to the Fortunates' plans.

Panspermia exploded in the Martian sky, sending massive burning rocks toward the surface. Though they never struck the city, fear gripped the hearts of all inhabitants in Ecopolis and Tropaion—especially the Fortunates, who watched the impure deliver a major blow to their universe. Worse still, the battle wasn't over.

The Fortunates redirected their focus to the group heading toward Goliath, overwhelmed with concern about their lack of preparation. The Stealthlord Fighters began attacking Apollo before separating to target Goliath's energy-generating transponders. The four remaining shuttles released cables from their underbellies, restraining every limb of the Golden Guardian before hurling it toward the portal's void. Icon realized too late that he had ordered the portal to be fully operational.

Instead of causing an explosion as planned, Apollo passed through the functional gateway as the shuttles released their cables and retreated. One shuttle, its wing entangled in the cord, followed Apollo through the portal.

The Stealthlord fighters continued their assault on the transponders without hesitation. When the final transponder exploded, the massive ring collapsed, destroying the gateway.

There was no time to celebrate—the retreating ships immediately encountered a swarm of Arrow Fighters. Though the Stealthlords were combat-ready, the shuttles were not. They were destroyed one by one until only two Stealthlords remained to race back to Earth.

On Mars, the phrase repeated endlessly: everything had been carefully planned for years leading to this moment, "The Day of Decimation," but the universe had different plans. No one could have predicted their adversaries would become even more powerful that day.

The Fortunates hadn't lost everything. The Battalion soldiers had claimed many Earthling lives before Kane and his team departed, only then did the tide turn as the Apostles joined the fight. The Fortunates now understood that most Earthlings lacked the Apostles' capabilities, and if Mars were invaded, the Endicots and Battalion could handle Earth's general population. This inspired plans for a second Battalion strike, provided they could distract the Apostles.

Luther recognized this threat—to save as many people as possible, they needed to accelerate their next strike against the Fortunates to slow Battalion production. The Fortunates, viewing the Battalion as mere machines, cared nothing for losses. Their goal wasn't expanding their empire but rather eliminating their opposition entirely through steady decimation until achieving full extinction. This made them particularly dangerous—they sought neither to integrate societies nor take control, but to commit complete genocide.

And now more than ever, revenge coursed through the Fortunates' blood. The destruction of the portal leaving no escape, coupled with the loss of Panspermia—their sustainable vessel for extended journeys—pushed the Fortunates to escalate the war. Perhaps it was also their predicament of having only Oculus Dexter as an escape route. Zeus, though enormous and equipped with temporary dwellings, wasn't designed for long excursions. Suddenly, the Fortunates found themselves fighting for survival.

The war raged on. Zeus hovering above Earth caused constant concern, but everyone knew it was needed back on Fortuna—the reason they'd always hesitated to use the giant. Would the loss of Goliath change their plans? No one knew for certain, but the Fortunates showed signs of desperation—a dangerous development for the Earthlings. A desperate enemy takes desperate measures. For now, they faced constant air strikes as Arrow Fighters conducted endless raids. These proved largely futile as the Apostles easily anticipated and destroyed the warplanes. The attacks served mainly to keep Earth's forces on guard and remind them of Zeus's looming presence, as it housed the seemingly endless supply of Arrows arriving from Mars. This also indicated the Battalion's production was growing exponentially. Fortunately, the Vatican and Apostles Hall—Earth's two most famous structures and symbols of strength and survival—remained well-guarded, giving Earthlings reason to believe and fight.

And fight they did. Each day of survival reminded the Fortunates of their previous world. Little did they know the Bacchians lurked among them, still unrevealed. This time, however, turmoil plagued their own planet. Unlike Fortuna, where citizens united in their belief in purity and the righteousness of eliminating lesser beings, Mars was different. These transplanted Earthlings had lost loved ones to the Fortunates. While Magnus maintained general control, some resisted—with Veracity often behind it. He pursued every lead, including investigating a minor atmospheric disturbance near the old mining tunnels outside Ecopolis.

What followed was a series of events leading to our present day. Some would say everything led to this, reaching back thousands of years—and they'd be right. No one exists independent of previous events, yet perhaps it was all predetermined. The stars speak in strange ways, in languages we don't yet fully comprehend.

We can only interpret as best we know how, and wartime perhaps speaks most clearly. Without consulting Luther, Zachary implemented his plan to attack Mars and the Fortunates, theorizing that a full-force assault would force them to focus on defense rather than attacking Earth. His theory proved correct.

Nearly a hundred Stealthlords soared into Earth's skies, accompanied by shuttles filled with armed Earthlings, Tiburon, and the Apostles. They expected casualties—while the Stealthlords could fight, many shuttles couldn't, and they couldn't protect everyone from the Battalion-manned Arrows intent on destruction. Once regrouped, they continued toward Mars.

The remaining Arrows attempted direct strikes on Earth, but largely failed. Zachary and Cornelius combined their powers to ward off serious threats—Cornelius would jump back in time to detect incoming attacks, while Zachary used Earth's elements to strike down the would-be attackers.

Luther, though shocked by Zachary's lack of coordination, adapted to the situation. It was time to show the Fortunates that the Bacchians were present—their revelation would depend on Magnus's actions.

The 13th Legion reached the mines with minimal defenses, treating it as a routine investigation. Their guard was down, though it wouldn't have mattered either way. As they entered the dim tunnel, none could have anticipated what lurked within, even as Felle Ha's voice entered their minds.

Felle Ha repeatedly warned them to turn back, but no soldier voiced these warnings to their team, likely not understanding what was happening. Unknown to them, Felle Ha had eggs nesting in the tunnels. As previously explained, Bacchians never act aggressively by nature, but will do anything within their power to survive. When repeated warnings went unheeded, Felle Ha protected its nest. By the time the Legion realized the danger, it was too late.

In mere seconds, the 13 ceased to exist. When word reached Magnus, the Fortunates' focus shifted from the approaching Earthling threat. The Bacchians had revealed themselves.

BACCHIANS REVEALED

During the enemies' three-week journey toward Mars, most attention focused on setting up defenses. The Fortunates in Tropaion barely noticed

Magnus's activities within Ecopolis, concerned only with analyzing his loyalty and viability as an ally. Thus, Magnus handled the situation alone.

When communication from the Legion grew sparse, Magnus found it curious but didn't anticipate what would be revealed. The few human guards awaiting the Legion's return grew distracted by the delay. Eventually, the soldiers reported back to Magnus, and while he didn't immediately suspect the Bacchians, he recognized a potential threat lurking in the tunnels below.

Luther contacted Zachary about these developments, promising ground support when the Earthlings arrived. Though they might not realize it was the Bacchians yet, he assured them they would soon enough.

Luther urged Zachary to quickly develop a successful plan, emphasizing the need for communication. Understanding the metropolis's construction and its weaknesses, Luther stressed the importance of protecting Ecopolis's population through careful action. He needed to inform Zachary about the semi-rebellious population within Ecopolis—these were still Earthlings who, whether through intentional blissfulness or ignorance, had missed the Fortunates' true plans from the beginning.

Thankfully, Zachary understood— many might not have survived otherwise. While Luther felt time standing still, events unfolded rapidly. As a typically methodical person who considered the impact of every action, Luther now had no choice but to trust the universe was guiding his decisions.

Magnus ordered a Battalion to search the tunnels for the 13th Legion, with human soldiers following behind. When they encountered the Bacchians, the humans knew they couldn't compete with what they witnessed. Despite their menacing features, the Bacchians' voices tried to comfort the humans, promising no harm. Multiple Bacchians whispering in their minds made the experience even more intimidating. The time for waiting had passed—the Acolytes knew they must now reveal themselves. Once the Fortunates learned of their presence, they could finally pursue their mission: ending Fortunate tyranny and saving their own kind.

The humans rushed back to Magnus's residence, describing what they'd seen only as *creatures*. Unfamiliar with Bacchian history, some might have thought they were native Martian inhabitants, but regardless, a threat lurked below. Their hurried reports convinced Magnus he needed to alert the Fortunates immediately—despite the approaching threat from above, they needed to address what lay beneath.

Magnus rushed through Endicots Lair to the Golden Tower, demanding an audience with all High Fortunates, especially Icon and Agatha. One can only imagine their fear and disbelief upon hearing Magnus's report. Their greatest fear had materialized—the Bacchians were here.

Ajax burst out of Endicots Lair to prepare for battle. Questions multiplied: How had this happened? How long had the enemy been present? How many were there? Could more be hidden? Would they have time to prepare Oculus Dexter for departure?

The Earthlings were approaching too. How much did they know? The Fortunates faced countless questions with little time to answer. Irony filled the room—they had planned to come to this system, to commit genocide against *inferior creatures* on both sides of the portal. Now they faced the possibility that the Day of Decimation might be their own. How could the stars betray them? They were the pure ones, the superior species—had the universe and forefathers lied? The story differed greatly from what they'd been told. Sometimes, you are not what the universe planned.

While the Fortunates hastily reconsidered their identity and restructured their immediate plans, Magnus returned to his residence in Ecopolis, where Luther would pay him a visit. All was about to be exposed.

<u>I AM VERACITY</u>

Luther had claimed, and many believed him, that the outcomes were never his intent. But Magnus had been frantically assessing whether they were in immediate danger. How many Bacchians had made it here? And how did they arrive? He searched for any inconsistencies.

Luther continued to act as if he knew nothing, though he knew it was only a matter of time before his brother pieced it all together.

During this time, Del Bu Roc left Vesta and began its approach toward Mars. Magnus had been too distracted to pay close attention to Luther's behavior, but he did notice one thing—Luther showed no urgency, no shock, despite the unsettling situation that had just come to light.

Their conversation continued, but then the radar detected something in the area. Del Bu Roc had been identified on its path toward Mars. Under ordinary circumstances, Magnus would have dismissed it—it was organic, not mechanical. But memories stirred in him, reminding him of the incident just outside Ecopolis, when everyone had made the same mistaken assumption.

Determined, Magnus investigated thoroughly this time. It was clearly a lifeform—nothing like anything he'd encountered, yet unmistakably alive. And as the pieces clicked into place, a chilling realization struck him: it had been Luther who investigated the tunnels. It had been Luther guarding Apollo when the strange signal was first detected.

Magnus turned to Luther, disbelief in his eyes, though a part of him had suspected the truth all along. When he finally asked, *Are you Veracity?* it wasn't a question. It was an accusation.

Luther's response left no room for doubt.

Yes.

Magnus's thoughts spun wildly, and he staggered toward the door. Luther knew exactly what his brother intended to do, and he couldn't let it happen. If Magnus could betray him by siding with an alien race—whether or not he believed their blood was his own—then Luther had to choose where his own loyalty lay. It lay with Earth.

It lay with the people he loved—the family and friends he still cherished in Ecopolis, where he felt more trapped by destiny than chosen by it.

And so, Luther drove a dagger into Magnus's back.

Magnus stumbled out of his home, bleeding and disoriented, navigating the streets of Ecopolis. He pressed onward, through Endicot's Lair, and finally reached the Golden Tower. Inside, chaos reigned—indecision and fear gripped everyone.

But Magnus had no words for them. He forced himself into the war room, every breath labored, and with the last of his strength, he hit the release switch.

Zeus would be unleashed on Earth.

The quantum bomb had begun its countdown.

When Agatha and Icon—two of the Fortunates—realized what Magnus had done, they knew two things. First, there was only one way out: *Oculus Dexter*. Even if escape were possible, the second realization was far more dire, they didn't know which direction the enemy would strike from.

The tail of *Oculus Dexter*, embedded deep in Mars's surface, was the safest part of the vessel. But it could also become a deathtrap. If they couldn't complete the procedure in time— rising from Mars and reforming the dome—they would be stranded, surrounded by enemies.

And as Mars's sky turned ominously dark, and the ground beneath them swarmed with combatants, they knew their window for survival was closing fast.

DIASPORA

As events on Mars unfolded, Zachary and Cornelius watched Zeus take on a new form. Its limbs detached from its torso, the head separating with precision. That was when Zachary realized what had happened—Zeus had been activated. With an expression as unyielding as stone, he turned to Cornelius and said, *It's time, Cornelius*

Meanwhile, back on Earth, those who hadn't departed for Mars were unaware of Zeus's apocalyptic capabilities. However, they knew that whatever was happening in the sky above was no omen of peace. The atmosphere was thick with dread. Then, from the top of Fort Vatican, a piercing tintinnabulation rang out, summoning people from every direction. They gathered, desperate for answers, but there were none to be given, only orders.

Everyone was instructed to proceed to the grounds below the Vatican. What awaited them was astonishing: a vast underground city, hidden beneath the sacred structure above. It bore little resemblance to the Vatican that crowned it. Instead, this subterranean marvel teemed with technology far beyond what they had imagined. The city was alive, filled with lush vegetation, wildlife, and ecosystems reminiscent of the legendary Ark built by the Martians centuries before.

At first, many believed it to be a fallout shelter, a sanctuary from the cataclysm unfolding above. But the truth became clear when the massive doors sealed shut. This place was more than a refuge.

The ancient tomes of Old Earth had been gathered here, alongside the *Scrolls of Jacob*.

Then came a tremor, deep and ominous. The entire underground city began to shift, rising through the earth with unstoppable force. It burst through the Vatican above, shattering the once-sacred monument. From beneath the ruins, Leviathan emerged, a colossal machine, the last and greatest creation of Warlord. Years ago, the first fallen Guardian had lain outside the Vatican, but this time, the Guardian's successor had returned— not as a fallen relic, but as a living vessel of salvation.

Leviathan was their escape. And though they did not yet know it, this machine would also become their new home.

Even as the world outside seemed to crumble into chaos, Zachary and Cornelius remained calm, almost hopeful.

Throughout history, tales of ancient origins have been told—legends of beings from distant worlds shaping the course of life on Earth. It is now believed that these stories were not of Earth's beginnings at all, but echoes of the Martians' past. When those tales were passed down, their origins blurred, becoming misunderstood or lost altogether. In time, they were seen not as Martian memories but as Earth's myths—forgotten pieces of another world's truth.

Our minds are filled with the imprints of the past, shaping what we believe to be original ideas. Monuments, inventions, sciences—all are fragments of memories deeply embedded in us, reimagined as our own creations. This cycle repeats across the universe, a cosmic rhythm where stories intertwine and resurface.

Such is the importance of remembering history, for it is never truly lost—only waiting to be rediscovered. Even Noah's Ark carries a shadow of this truth. The Martians, long before Earth's flood myth, embarked on an ark of their own.

And now, once again, Zachary stood as a steward of life. He gathered his people, animals, and as many artifacts of their world as he could—books, scrolls, and the knowledge of the civilization they were leaving behind. Leviathan would carry them through the darkness, just as the ancient Ark had once carried life through the storm.

Leviathan

If not for Warlord's tremendous display of his gift, the human race might have ceased to exist. The wondrous contrivance was a sight to behold. Even the Fortunates would have been impressed, considering it was built mostly from the remnants of *Ares*—the same metals left behind when Ares failed to breach the Vatican's walls and fell to the Apostles. Thanks to its immense size and the technological framework embedded within the Guardian, the foundation for Leviathan was made possible. Additional metals were incorporated, but at its core, Leviathan's weaponry and heart came from Ares itself.

With his ability to reconstruct metals into functional machinery and weaponize them, Warlord created Leviathan. It lay hidden beneath the grounds of Fort Vatican, waiting for its moment. Zachary had always known that if Earth ever faced its demise, there would be a way for humanity to survive—and Leviathan was that way.

Leviathan was a vast spherical vessel, the size of a small city in circumference, and five levels deep.

When it appeared in the sky above Mars during the war, it was as though a star of hope ignited in the eyes of every displaced Earthling. As Luther led the people toward the great fuselage for their exodus from the red planet, they no longer cared where they were headed. Upon entering, they marveled at what lay before them and immediately embraced it as home.

The floating city, traveling across the universe, soon developed its own regions and neighborhoods. Inside its vast environment, distinctive landmarks emerged—a zoo housing wildlife and the simulated Snake Room, reminiscent of the one in the Vatican. Great Throne Mountain stood proudly, now complemented by a pergola structure echoing those of the Roman Empire. A grand library housed ancient writings alongside the Scrolls of Jacob.

At the top level, a room dedicated to the Apostles displayed sculptures salvaged from the ruins of the Vatican. These relics, along with plaques recounting the Apostles' tales, ensured their legacy endured. Those born aboard Leviathan, as well as those from the two worlds once orbiting Copernicus, quickly adapted to their new life. The only difference was that Leviathan sailed through the expanse of space—with no sun to orbit and no sky above, only the gaze of a virtual one.

Husen
12.23

As Zeus began its descent toward Earth, an attempt was made to intercept its head before impact and carry it toward their ancient enemies. It was no easy task, but one they had to undertake. The engines of Leviathan slowed just enough to align with the projectile's path, but the head of Zeus still hurtled past them—seemingly lost.

That's when Cornelius made his move. His ability to jump back in time, though limited to brief increments, was exactly what they needed. With bursts of light and arcs of electricity surging from his body, Cornelius leapt. Now aware of the projectile's trajectory, they successfully intercepted the head. With the massive cranium, still harboring its incendiary device, secured aboard Leviathan, their mission continued.

Leviathan, now carrying the head of Zeus, hurtled toward Mars, determined to return the Guardian to its creators. Although the enormous head might have been cumbersome for other vessels, it posed no obstacle for Leviathan. Unfazed and resolute, the massive ship pressed onward through the void, destined to confront its past.

GENOCIDE

While it was a cause for celebration, having accomplished the impossible, they looked back and saw their precious home slowly implode. With a final gesture of farewell, Earth was no more—reduced to a mere memory for all of us. But this was only the beginning of the end for the two worlds that had waged a war generations in the making.

Battalion Arrows raced out to secure the skies over Mars, with far more fighters than anyone could have imagined filling the heavens above. Meanwhile, Endicots gathered within Endicots' Lair and Tropaion, bracing for the inevitable ground assault that was sure to follow.

At the same time, Oculus Dexter prepared to extract from the surface of

Mars, with little regard for those still clinging to life in Ecopolis. What was once a time of hope for the transplanted Earthlings now faded into uncertainty. They began to wonder what would become of them. They were ill-prepared to live as a self-reliant society, having built their lives around dependence on the Fortunates—including for their defense.

The Martians were unaware of Earth's demise or the existence of Leviathan. But when they looked to the stars, they saw streaks of light flashing across the sky—Earthlings had arrived. Their Battalion soldiers in Arrow Fighters clashed with the Stealthlord fighters, igniting the long dreaded confrontation.

Without a docking station in orbit, as was the norm with Panspermia, the Earthlings maneuvered close to Mars's atmosphere. The Stealthlords fought desperately to ensure as many shuttles as possible reached the surface, where Tiburon and the Apostles led the charge. Upon landing, little could be seen from Ecopolis. With Zachary and the scrolls aboard Leviathan, it was understood that the Apostles would strike between Endicots' Lair and Tropaion—Mars's most vulnerable point, according to Luther's counsel. Their attack would also prevent Oculus Dexter from rising.

The Apostles inflicted heavy damage, clearing the way for the Earthlings to storm Endicots' Lair and engage the formidable warriors defending it. Though the Fortunates had taken refuge within Tropaion, the Endicots fought fiercely, slaughtering Earthlings by the dozens. Even the Apostles could not stop Ajax, who fought with relentless fury. When he killed Gravitas, it became clear that his rage was unstoppable—his determination to preserve his bloodline unwavering. With Jupiter in his grip, Ajax struck with terrifying precision, and the Endicots began to regain control of their territory.

In the chaos, it was difficult to determine where the new Martians stood or who might emerge as their savior—if one existed at all. The desperate citizens could do nothing but wait, unsure whether their fate would bring salvation or doom.

Then Luther rose, holding the mask of Veracity high. "I *am* Veracity," he proclaimed. "Do not fear—others are coming to save you." He declared that the aliens the Fortunates had so feared were here, not as monsters but as allies, and that this war would be won to preserve Earthling life.

At that moment, an effulgent figure burst through the darkened sky: Del Bu Roc had arrived. It tore through the atmosphere, obliterating the Battalion soldiers attempting to reach their Arrow Fighters and making its way toward Tropaion. From afar, consternation rippled through the city. At the foot of the Golden Tower, the Bacchians emerged from underground, poised to infiltrate the Fortunates' temple of power.

Del Bu Roc pierced a hole through Tropaion's dome. The rupture crippled the city's defenses, but the Bacchians were only slowed. Their unique respiratory systems allowed them to filter and adapt to the compromised atmosphere. While the Fortunates suffered, the Bacchians pressed on. If not for the atmospheric generator sustaining the remaining environment, the Fortunates would have fallen even faster.

The G.O.D.S. delayed the extermination of the High Fortunates—but only temporarily. Unfamiliar with their opponents, the Bacchians failed to realize that Kane was missing from battle. Some still speculate whether the Fortunates were completely annihilated, or if rumors of survivors fleeing toward Ecopolis were mere hearsay. Nonetheless, the Bacchians decimated the G.O.D.S., leaving their severed heads at the doors of the tower.

From that point forward, the Bacchians executed every Fortunate they found in Tropaion. As Darrd watched, they beheaded each one, exposing the micro-biotic secrets stored within their craniums. It is said that Darrd himself removed the heads of Icon and Agatha, leaving the remaining Fortunates leaderless—without king or queen, and without the option to surrender.

The massacre spilled into the streets of Tropaion. Though few survived to witness the horror, Earthlings from Endicots' Lair and Bacchians alike later recounted the brutality—how the Acolytes ran rampant, beheading and dismembering the populace as Del Bu Roc bombarded the city from above. In Ecopolis, the people could do nothing but listen to the distant screams echoing through the domes.

At the time, the Acolytes were unaware of Leviathan's arrival. Had they known, it would have changed little; their rampage would have continued regardless. When the time came, Luther urged Darrd and the others to evacuate.

The end of the Fortunates came with grim finality. Ajax, the fiercest among them, was struck down—not by an enemy, but by his own weapon. Dementia, one of the Apostles, clouded his mind with dark thoughts, giving Masquerade the opening she needed. She approached Ajax, and with a single touch, absorbed not only his appearance but his strength. Distracted by the illusions in his mind, Ajax was helpless as she wrestled Jupiter from his grasp and drove it into his chest. The last thing he saw was his own face, reflected back at him as Masquerade delivered the fatal blow. One could only imagine that he was witnessing exactly what Peter had in his final moments. With cold precision, she severed Ajax's platinum head from his body, leaving his lifeless eyes wide open—filled with disbelief, as though he still searched the universe for a purpose unfulfilled.

When Leviathan arrived, it heralded the end of yet another world. The massive vessel hovered above Mars, extending its paths to the floating city.

With great urgency, Luther called upon all in Ecopolis to board. Zachary and Cornelius waved from above, welcoming the Martians—now Earthlings once more—into the embrace of humankind.

As they ascended, the remaining Acolytes boarded Del Bu Roc, satisfied that all High Fortunates within the tower had been accounted for. Though Adom was never found, the Bacchians dismissed the oversight—it no longer mattered.

Once Leviathan reached a safe distance from Mars, the head of Zeus was released. It plummeted toward the planet, striking the shattered dome of Tropaion and triggering the collapse of the remaining cities—Endicots' Lair and Ecopolis included. From their vantage point aboard Leviathan, the survivors watched as the atmospheric-controlled domes crumbled, and Mars met the same fate as Earth.

It is a tragic irony that the life of a planet must end because of those who claim it as their own—when all it ever did was welcome those who inhabited it.

DENOUEMENT

It is now twenty-five After M.E. (Mars and Earth), the latest calendar we follow since our travels began. Though we no longer revolve around the Sun, we measure time in EBR (Earth-Based Revolutions) to stay aligned with the memory of our home world and the universe's rhythm. Even with Earth reduced to dust and Mars a fractured remnant adrift in space— possibly on its way to becoming four asteroids orbiting Copernicus—we hold onto their significance. What matters is not the places they were but the lessons they carry.

Their stories are warnings, as relevant as they are tragic. If we allow these stories to become myths or mere parables, they will lose their power. History must remain alive in us, not just as fact, but as insight—because the truth is malleable, shaped by who tells it and when. The legacy of Mars and Earth is more than distant ruins or lost civilizations; it is a lesson in balance. When energy within us falls out of sync with the universe, both will suffer.

Onboard the *Leviathan*, our sojourning nation adrift in the cosmos, we still seek closure to the chapter Mars and Earth began. If we reach the worlds of Fortuna or Bacchus, perhaps the answers will await us, though we fear these worlds too may lie in ruin, casualties of wars that rage beyond our reach. Did the Earth shuttle cross into their system before the destruction of Goliath? What new ripples did that collision cause in the unfolding war? Even if we reach them, there is no certainty that answers remain.

Memory cell enhancement efforts continue within *Leviathan*, led by scientists like Darrd. Yet, we only grasp fragments of our history, especially the enigmatic transition from Mars to Earth. What we know is limited—Martians fleeing their home world before it suffered it's dissolved atmosphere, embedding what they could in Earth's early civilizations. But much remains shrouded, lost between migrations, mythologies, and broken timelines. Attempts to recover lost memories through electrical stimulation or mnemonic research have revealed only glimpses of that ancient knowledge.

Religions, myths, and names—once known truths—have shifted over millennia. Terra became Earth; the moon, once called Mimas, was forgotten. Even the Sun itself was known as Copernicus, though such names now sound like distant fables. Were these changes a natural evolution or the result of deliberate alteration during tumultuous times like the Ice Age? Why do all religions tell the same stories in different ways? Were they remnants of Martian knowledge passed down through Earth's fragmented ages?

These questions remain open, but what we do know is this: Our survival depends on remembering. If history falls into the hands of those with selfish motives, it will be rewritten to suit their needs. In each tale, there are steppingstones to the next chapter—markers on the path that must be carried forward. Though madness may lurk in the pursuit of truth, there is no greater task than to retain what came before and pass it onward, unaltered by fear or convenience.

I write these words as a reminder. Leviathan continues its journey, carrying memories of what was lost. Even as significant individuals like Luther remain with us—though he now spends much of his time among the Acolytes on Del Bu Roc—we sense how fragile these memories are. Already, those born aboard Leviathan lose sight of the magnitude of Earth and Mars, forgetting how closely connected their fate is to our own.

I was only five years old when Ecopolis was torn from me, when we were interrogated by those Earthlings who remained. *What role did you play?* they asked. "Could you have done more?" We were eventually reintegrated into society, but suspicions lingered—suspicions that some of us might be Fortunates, that some Fortunates might have hidden among us aboard *Leviathan*. Although those investigations have long since ended, whispers persist—rumors of disappearances during the questioning, fates that will likely become mere footnotes in the annals of history.

Conflict is inevitable. But understanding why conflicts arise is half the battle. By recalling the past, we may change the outcome, steering events toward a more just resolution. The search for a new home continues, but we ask ourselves: Will the worlds of Fortuna and Bacchus still stand? Have they already been claimed by others? And even if we find them intact, can we sustain what lies ahead, just as the ancients of old—Patience and Fortitude—did on their initial migration?

As we voyage deeper into uncharted space, delays have plagued our journey. We know that the Omniscient One had the gift of clairvoyance, but each of us carries the ability to glimpse the past through the memories encoded in our DNA. However, this path is treacherous. Memories passed through generations blur, becoming dreams or déjà vu—experiences dismissed too easily. If we erase history from our surroundings, it will fade from our minds, leaving us vulnerable to those who would reshape the narrative to their advantage.

Without history, future generations will have no compass, no anchor to ground their identity. They will not know what they are fighting for. And the cycle will repeat. That is why I write—to remind, to preserve. *Leviathan* presses onward, its people referred to by some as *Leviathanians*, by others as *Expedities*. We are the chroniclers of our age, carrying forward the burden of history.

This story is not yet complete, for each moment is but a steppingstone to the next. We do not know what trials or discoveries that await us. But we will record them. We will remember them. And from these records, the next chapter will unfold—another page in the endless story of the universe. We can only hope that a chronicle of Alpha-Centauri will await us and help piece together the puzzle that is our universe.

I am but one messenger for this passage, sharing all that I know of this story. Please, pass this book forward and add anything I may have inadvertently missed or was not told. For every ending is but the beginning of another chapter, as the story of this vast and boundless universe continues to unfold— today, tomorrow, and even yesterday. ~Iasol 1:2